'I want to dance with the sexiest woman here and show them she's mine.'

'I'm not yours. Only in name.'

Even as Grace spoke the words she knew them to be a lie. Luca had imprinted himself indelibly onto every one of her senses.

He leaned into her and spoke into her neck. 'You will *always* be mine.'

He felt so warm, his touch penetrating her skin and dancing into the very fabric of her being. The stars that resided in the midnight of his eyes gleamed, holding her gaze, trapping her in their depths.

He brushed his lips against her neck, nipping at the sensitive skin. 'Dance with me.'

Luca was like a drug to her. She could survive without him, but it was like breathing air with only a fraction of the usual oxygen.

She hated him.

She loved him.

The two sides were interchangeable.

The only constant she felt was desire. And she was sick of fighting it and pushing it away. There could only ever be one outcome.

'Yes,' she breathed, 'I'll dance with you.'

THE IRRESISTIBLE SICILIANS

Dark-hearted men, with devastating appeal!

These powerful Sicilian men are
bound by years of family legacies and dark secrets.

But now the power rests with them.

No *man* would dare challenge
these hot-blooded Sicilians…

But their women are another matter!

Have these world-renowned Sicilians met their match?

Read Luca Mastrangelo's story in:
WHAT A SICILIAN HUSBAND WANTS
March 2014

Read Pepe Mastrangelo's story in:
THE SICILIAN'S UNEXPECTED DUTY
April 2014

And look out for Francesco Calvetti's story
coming soon!

WHAT A SICILIAN HUSBAND WANTS

BY

MICHELLE SMART

Published in Great Britain 2014
by Mills & Boon, an imprint of Harlequin (UK) Limited,
Eton House, 18-24 Paradise Road, Richmond, Surrey, TW9 1SR

ISBN: 978 0 263 24185 3

Harlequin (UK) Limited's policy is to use papers that are natural, renewable and recyclable products and made from wood grown in sustainable forests. The logging and manufacturing processes conform to the legal

Printed and
by CPI Ant

Michelle Smart's love affair with books began as a baby, when she would cuddle them in her cot. This love for all things wordy has never left her. A voracious reader of all genres, her love of romance was cemented at the age of twelve when she came across her first Mills & Boon® book. That book sparked a seed and, although she didn't have the words to explain it then, she discovered something special—that a book had the capacity to make her heart beat as if she were falling in love.

When not reading, or pretending to do the housework, Michelle loves nothing more than creating worlds of her own featuring handsome, brooding heroes and the sparkly, feisty women who can melt their frozen hearts. She hopes her books can make her readers' hearts beat a little faster too.

Michelle Smart lives in Northamptonshire with her own hero and their two young sons.

Recent titles by the same author:

THE RINGS THAT BIND

For Luke with all my love.

CHAPTER ONE

GRACE REACHED THE bottom of the stairs and padded barefoot to the alarm on the wall. Working on autopilot, she punched in the code and disabled it along with the sensors running throughout the ground floor. Only once had she forgotten to deactivate it. She had still been half asleep, little more than a zombie. By the time she had walked into the kitchen, the house was making more noise than a dozen hen parties trapped in a large room consuming vast quantities of Jaeger Bombs.

She switched the kettle on and yawned loudly.

Coffee. That was what she needed—a strong dose of caffeine and a good blast of sugar.

While waiting for the kettle to boil, she pulled back the insulating curtains covering the back door and peeked through the pane of glass. Bright early-morning sunlight temporarily blinded her. Squinting, she was greeted with the sight of a thick layer of frost covering the garden. It made her skin feel cold just looking at it. She dropped the curtain sharpish.

Still shivering, she turned to the kitchen table and switched the laptop on. Leaving it to boot up, she made her coffee, adding a huge dollop of milk to cool it down quicker. She brought the mug to her lips and was about to take her first sip when the doorbell rang.

A chill that had nothing to do with the cold outside swept through her, seeping into her bones.

Every hair on her body stood to attention.

Her heart crashed against her ribs, the motion strong enough to unbalance her and slosh hot coffee over her hand and fingers.

She winced and muttered an oath, but the slight scald did her good. It snapped her to attention.

Shoving the mug on the counter, spilling more coffee in the process, she wiped her smarting hand on her dressing gown and strode to the tall cupboard in the corner. She pulled out a wicker basket, burrowed a hand under the pile of tea towels and reached for the small, cold handgun.

The doorbell rang out a second time.

The laptop now booted and ready to use, she clicked on the icon that connected to the live feed from the four surveillance cameras covering the perimeter of her house. The screen split into quarters. Only the top right-hand frame showed anything out of the ordinary.

She didn't recognise the small figure wrapped in the thick parka, woolly hat and matching scarf. The woman's knees were springing slightly and she clutched a large bag to her belly, no doubt trying to keep warm in the icy conditions.

Torn between a hard-wired wariness towards strangers and feeling sorry for the freezing woman, Grace walked cautiously down the narrow hallway and drew back the heavy curtain covering the front door. The muffled shape was opaque through the frosted glass panel. Holding the gun securely behind her back with her right hand, she fumbled open the three sliding locks, unlocked the deadbolt and loosened the safety chain. Only then did she turn the lock and pull the door one and a half inches, the exact amount of slack given by the chain.

'Sorry to bother you,' the woman said, her teeth chattering. She raised her phone. 'My car has broken down. Can I borrow your phone to call my husband, please? I can't get a signal on my mobile.'

Not surprising, Grace thought. Most of the mobile networks struggled for a signal in this small Cornish village. Luckily, her landline worked fine.

She perused the stranger for longer than was polite. The woman was a good four inches shorter than Grace and, beneath the thick clothing, only a slight thing. What she could see of her face was red from the cold.

Rationally she knew this stranger could not pose a threat. Even so…

Even so, her mind raced as she thought of a whole posse of reasons as to why it was impossible to let her in to make her call and then offer the hospitality of warmth from the ever-constant cast-iron cooker in the kitchen.

Much as she knew she should slam the door in the stranger's face and direct her to the farmhouse at the top of the drive, she could not bring herself to be so uncharitable. It would be at least another ten-minute walk for the poor thing.

'Hold on a sec,' she said, shutting the door. She stuffed the gun into the deep pocket of her dressing gown, a place she knew topped the list of most stupid places to hide a firearm. She had no choice but to place it there.

Stupid, paranoid mind. You've been hiding for too long. Can't even open a door without expecting an ambush.

She unlocked the chain and opened the door.

'Thank you so much,' the woman said, stepping straight in and stamping her feet on the welcome mat to shake off the early-morning frost clinging to them. 'I was starting to think I'd never find civilisation. The roads around here are dreadful.'

Grace forced a polite smile and shut the door behind her. The cold had already rushed into the heavily insulated house. A cold, uneasy feeling swept through her, a feeling she disregarded.

'The phone's right here,' she said, indicating the landline on the small table by the front door. 'Help yourself.'

The woman lifted the receiver and made her call, pressing a finger to her ear and speaking in a low murmur.

The conversation went on for a good few minutes. When she finished, the woman put the receiver back on the cradle and smiled at Grace. The smile didn't quite meet her eyes. 'Thanks for that. I'll get out of your hair now.'

'You're welcome to wait here for your husband,' Grace said, hating the thought of anyone being outside in such awful conditions.

'No. I need to go. He won't be long.'

'Are you sure? It's horrid out there.'

The woman backed up to the front door and reached for the handle. 'I'm sure. Thank you.' She opened the door and headed off down the driveway without so much as a goodbye.

Perplexed, Grace stared at the rapidly retreating figure for a few seconds before shutting the door and relocking it.

She shivered.

The hairs on her arms were standing to attention again.

It took a few beats before she recognised the coldness in her bones as a warning and not a pure physical reaction.

Something was off...

Standing stock-still, she strained her ears. The only noise she could detect was the thundering of her own blood careering through her at the rate of knots.

Stupid, paranoid mind.

All the same, something about the stranger's demeanour played on her mind. As she padded back to the kitchen, all she could think about was the way the woman had rushed off…

The shock of the doorbell ringing a short while earlier was nothing compared to the floor-rooting terror of finding the tall, darkly handsome man in her kitchen, a man flanked by two gorilla-resembling goons.

'Wait in the car for me,' he said to them, not taking his eyes off Grace.

The goons left immediately, departing through the back door, the same door that had been locked just ten minutes earlier…

'Good morning, *bella*.'

Bella. The way that one particular word tripped off his tongue like a caress paralysed her. The drumming in her heart was instantaneous, a memory flickering back to life at the first sound of his voice. A beautiful, velvety rich voice with a heavy Sicilian accent that made his English sing.

The drumming became a loud pump. The paralysis was replaced with a fizzing energy that cleared her head of the fog that had filled it. Without taking her eyes off him, she slid her hand into her pocket and pulled out the gun.

'I'm going to give you five seconds to get out of my house.'

Only by the tiniest flicker of a thick black eyebrow did Luca react to having a gun aimed at his chest. His firm lips twitched as he lazily placed his hands in the air. 'Or what? You'll shoot me?'

'Don't move,' she snapped, her eyes widening as, hands held aloft, he took a step towards her. 'Get back!'

It could almost be described as humorous that Luca, unarmed, was utterly unfazed while she, holding a lethal weapon in her hands, was cold with fear.

She doubted he had ever felt a solitary jolt of fear in his life.

She must not let panic control her. She had always known this day would come. Mentally and physically she had prepared for it.

'I said get back.' She tried to steady her grip on the gun but her hands were trembling so hard she had to use all her concentration to keep the aim straight.

'Is this how you greet all your guests, *bella*?' He cocked his head to one side and took another step towards her, then another, his deep-set eyes not moving from her face. At some point she had forgotten how mesmerising they were, how the thick black lashes framed eyes so dark she had once believed them to be black. Only upon the closest of inspections could a person see they were in fact a deep, dark blue, like a clear summer's night. And once you knew their colour you never forgot.

How vividly she recalled the first time she had seen those eyes close up. That had been the point when every cell of her body had come alive. That had been the point she had fallen helplessly in love.

But that had been a long time ago. Any love she felt for him had died ten months ago when the truth about him could no longer be denied.

'Only the uninvited ones.' Deliberately she made a big show of slipping the safety catch off the gun. 'I will tell you one last time, get out of my house.'

He had inched close enough for her to see the pulse in his temple throb. She had to get him out of the house *right now.*

'Put the gun away, Grace. You have no idea how to handle such a dangerous weapon.'

Having a gun pointed at him had not figured in any of the welcomes Luca had been expecting. His heart thundered beneath his chest and, while he did not believe she would shoot him, the last thing he wanted was to panic her into doing something beyond either of their control.

He could hardly credit that he had found her. Finally.

As soon as he had positively identified her photo, he had boarded the jet kept on permanent standby for this very purpose, and travelled straight to England.

Grace's face was void of expression. 'You have no idea what I'm capable of handling. How did you find me?'

Somehow he managed to quell the spike of rage her toneless words provoked. She could be speaking to a stranger for all the emotion she conveyed. 'With great difficulty. Now put the gun down. I only want to talk to you. Nothing more.'

She made no attempt to hide her incredulity. 'You came all this way and went to all this trouble just so you could *talk* to me? If you just wanted to talk, why not knock on the door like a normal person rather than get a stooge to distract me so you can break in through the back door?'

'Because, my clever, deceitful Grace, you have led me on a merry dance around Europe. You have gone to incredible lengths to hide from me.' So successful had she been in keeping one step ahead, he'd been ready to believe she had a magic portal to vanish with whenever he got too close. Even before he'd verified the picture was truly her, he had insisted his men keep a close watch on the house with instructions to follow her if she went anywhere. Just in case. He would not let her slip through his fingers again.

'I haven't led you anywhere. If I had wanted you to find me I would have given directions.' Keeping hold of the gun with her right hand, she wiped her left down the side of her thin dressing gown, the movement pulling it open.

Her detachment was all on the surface.

A heavy thickness settled in his blood. The long pyjama bottoms and matching vest top showed off her slender, almost androgynous figure beautifully. Yet there was something softer than he remembered about her physique, a softness not matched in the coolness of her unwavering hazel eyes.

His mouth ran dry. Wetting his lips with his tongue, he continued to scrutinise her.

She had changed so much. If he had crossed her in the street he would have likely not recognised her. This, undoubtedly, had been her intention.

He had almost disregarded the photo. It had been taken mere minutes after his men arrived and strategically placed themselves out of sight of her security cameras. She had left the house for a few moments to collect her post from the box at the bottom of her driveway, bundled up in a thick, shapeless coat. They had managed to fire off a couple of shots before she had gone back inside but only one had captured part of her face.

The angle of her head had caught his attention. As he'd studied it closely a flicker in his belly had ignited. It was Grace. It was the same angle she always tilted her head when thinking, the same angle she would strike when standing in front of a large canvas with a paintbrush in her mouth. Of course, in those days, her hair had been long. And blonde. Not the short, red pixie haircut she now sported. It was a style he should find abhorrent but on Grace he found strangely compelling. Sexy.

Very sexy.

'How was I supposed to know you didn't want to be found?' he asked coolly. 'You left without a word to me or anyone. You didn't even have the courtesy to leave a note.'

'I would have thought my silence made it clear.'

Her silence had spoken volumes. But how could he not search for her? He would have searched for ever.

This was the woman who had promised to love and honour him until death did they part, not until…

That was the precise problem. He had no idea why she had simply vanished from his life.

And he could hardly credit he was now standing less than ten feet from her.

'You didn't take any of your clothes.' She hadn't taken anything. She had gone for a walk on the estate, climbed over the fence that marked the perimeter and vanished.

'Your goons would have been suspicious if I'd wandered through the vineyard with a ruddy great suitcase.'

Was that really sarcasm he detected in her voice? From Grace?

'I knew you would try to find me. That's why I have a gun—to stop you or your men from forcing me to return. Because I tell you now, I am not setting foot in Sicily again. So, unless you want to learn for yourself how good my aim is, I suggest you leave. And put your hands back up where I can see them.'

For a moment all he could do was stare in disbelief. 'What the hell happened to you?'

This was not the happy-go-lucky artist he had known and loved, the woman who had always looked at him with such happiness. He had long been accustomed to women looking at him with lust—devotion even. No one could ever accuse Grace of something as insipid as devotion yet she was the only woman who had ever made him feel her world was a better, happier place just for him being in it. She was the only woman who had ever made *his* world a happier place for being in it.

By contrast, this woman's eyes conveyed nothing but cold, hard contempt. It was like looking into the eyes of a stranger.

The wife he knew did not exist any more. Not for him.

Maybe she was the same old Grace when in the company of friends. Maybe she could still warm a cold room with a smile.

But not for him.

Her icy voice broke through the sudden haze clouding his vision. 'You know what they say: marry in haste, repent at leisure. Well, I have done nothing but repent since I left you.'

Long-ago uttered words floated back to him. *'I love you more than anyone or anything. I belong to you, Luca. We belong to each other.'*

His stomach heaved. He sucked in air through his nostrils, breathing deeply to quell the nausea lining his throat.

This was not his wife.

He should turn around and walk away but he deserved answers.

And he would have them. If he had to tie her to a chair for a month he would get the truth out of her.

'I'll ask you one more time—how did you find me?' She repeated her earlier question through gritted teeth.

'With the help of your friend's phone.'

For the first time her composure dropped, her jaw slackening. 'Cara?'

'Yes.'

'I don't believe you. Cara would never betray me.'

'She didn't. Her phone did. You called her on it shortly after you left me.'

Her face whitened. 'She would never have given it to you.'

'No,' he agreed, experiencing a surge of satisfaction at having broken through her cool façade. 'I regret that underhand methods were used to obtain it from her, but once we had it in our possession it was simple enough to find your number and, from that, your location.'

He made it sound so straightforward. Instead, his initial jubilation at getting her number had been doused. Her network provider had no way of getting a fix on her—her phone was not being used, had likely been thrown away or destroyed. Another dead end. Or so it had seemed until a week ago when it had unexpectedly sprung back to life. Luckily, he'd paid someone from the network to keep a watch on the number in case a miracle occurred.

It seemed miracles did happen.

'Does Cara know what you did?'

'I don't know.' He didn't care. What he did care about was the way Grace's hands were shaking. Shaking hands and guns were not a good combination. 'Give me the gun or put it down.'

'No.' She raised it higher, her eyes widening. 'I'm not putting this down until you leave. Get out of my house.'

'I'm not going anywhere, so you might as well put it down.' He kept his tone calm and took a step towards her.

'Get away from me,' she said, stepping back, her voice rising. 'Don't come any closer.'

'We both know you won't shoot me.' He lowered one of his raised hands and extended it towards her, the tips of his fingers closing in on the barrel of the gun.

'I said get away from me!' Her words came out as a screech and were immediately followed by the loud tone of his phone ringing out in his pocket.

Like a tightly coiled spring suddenly released, Grace jumped at the sound.

In the confines of the small cottage, the noise of the gun was deafening, loud enough to distract him from the bee sting on his right shoulder.

They stood in frozen silence until Grace's chest shuddered and she dropped the gun to the stone floor. It landed with a loud clang, the only noise apart from the ringing in his ears.

He had only a snapshot of time to register her white-faced shock before the wet warmth on his shoulder demanded his attention. Pulling the top of his jacket aside, he winced as a burn of pain went through him. His disbelief at the red fluid seeping through his white shirt was nothing compared to his shock when he finally comprehended that the distant ringing in his ears was not an echo from the gunshot but the wails of a baby.

She had shot him.

Dear God, she had shot him.

Through her ringing ears she could hear Lily's distant wails, a noise that seemed as far away as the moon.

She had shot him.

Her hand flew to her mouth and Grace could do nothing but stare at the blood seeping out of Luca's right shoulder.

He stared back at her with a look that could only be described as stunned.

On legs that didn't belong to her, she hurried to him. Her cold blood chilled further. Up close, the wound looked even worse. She reached out a hand, pausing before she could touch him.

'I'm so sorry,' she said dumbly, trying to clear her head of the drum banging loudly in it. 'I'll get something for the bleeding.' Her stomach churning, Grace rushed to the tall cupboard. She pulled out the same basket in which she had stored that monstrous gun and grabbed some tea towels.

Lily's cries became more distressed, the piercing sound penetrating the thick walls of the cottage and striking through Grace's heart.

Dear God, what was she going to *do*?

Could Luca even hear the cries? Or had the shock of

being shot deafened him just as it had temporarily dulled her own senses?

He had sat down at the table. His olive skin had paled considerably, the dark stubble across his jawline pronounced.

This was the closest to vulnerable she had ever seen him.

She leaned over to place a clean towel against the wound. His uninjured hand shot up and grabbed her wrist. 'What do you think you are doing?'

'Trying to stem the blood flow.'

He ground his teeth together and leaned forward so their faces were just inches apart. 'I am quite capable of tending to my own injury. Leave it with me and tend to the baby you are hiding upstairs.'

CHAPTER TWO

AT LUCA'S MENACINGLY delivered words, all the blood running through Grace's veins plunged to her feet.

White light flickered behind her eyes before she caught a waft of warm, minty breath and an enormous shudder ran through her.

'Are you in immediate danger?' She managed to drag the question out, jerking her wrist against his grip.

'No.' If anything, his hold tightened.

'Then let go of me.'

Those midnight eyes flashed before he sprang his fingers open like a remote-controlled robot.

In a murky daze, she climbed the stairs and walked into the bedroom she shared with her twelve-week-old daughter.

Lily lay flat on her back in her cot. Her thin arms were struck out like a starfish, her little legs kicking in all directions, her cute face scrunched up and bright red. Grace had no doubt that if her tear ducts had developed, Lily's cheeks would be soaked.

Scooping her out of the cot, she brought her to her chest and breathed in her daughter's sweet, innocent scent. 'Oh, Lily, I'm so sorry,' she choked out, swaying gently as she tried to soothe her. 'Your mummy has done a terrible, terrible thing.'

The implications hit her with the force of a tsunami. As

she patted Lily's bottom and murmured words of comfort, her mind raced.

She had shot Luca. She had actually shot someone; a living person. She had caused physical harm to the man she had once loved, the same man who now knew of the existence of her child.

Inhaling Lily's scent brought some control to her careering thoughts, and the fogginess clouding her brain began to abate.

Under no circumstances could she let the shock of all that had just occurred control her actions. She needed to take control, now, before it was too late.

Too late?

Who was she trying to fool? Of course it was too late.

What did she expect? That Luca would take her shooting him and hiding the existence of their child on the chin and walk away?

And she'd so nearly got away with it.

She'd managed to get hold of the gun only a couple of months ago, when she had been unable to sleep for fear of Luca's men finding them and tearing Lily away from her. She had seen the evidence of what her husband was capable of, evidence that burned her retinas and flourished in her nightmares.

The threat of prison if she were caught with an illegal firearm had not deterred her from purchasing it. She'd got it from the son of the farmer she rented the cottage from, a young man with a few unsavoury acquaintances. She hadn't cared where it came from; she was safer with it. Lily was safer with it. Knowing it was in the house allowed her to sleep. Sometimes.

Luca's men were always armed. And they were dangerous. Prison had seemed preferable to falling into their clutches.

They were also stupid. She had outwitted them before when she made her escape. She could outwit them again.

Except Luca had come for her personally, something she had not anticipated. She had imagined him like a king in his castle, waiting for his soldiers to bring his erring queen home, so she could be locked in the tower for the rest of her days.

Luca was not stupid. Luca was the sharpest person she had ever known, which made him infinitely more dangerous than his lackeys, and much harder to outwit.

Some sixth sense had been nagging at her for weeks that it was time to move on. Why, oh, why had she not acted on it sooner?

Prison did now loom dark. Not a traditional cell of iron bars and a tiny slot for a window, but a towering pink sandstone nightmare.

Lily finally stopped whimpering. Soothed and snug, she fixed her trusting, night-blue eyes on her mummy.

Her mummy, Grace reminded herself. This was not just about her—this was about her innocent, dependent child. The first time she had held her alone, away from the ears of midwives and obstetricians, Grace had made her daughter a promise. She had sworn she would keep her safe.

She had sworn she would never let her fall into the hands of the dangerous gangster that was Lily's father.

It was amazing how long Grace was able to drag out washing and dressing into a pair of faded jeans and a long, thick purple jumper. By the time she had changed Lily's nappy and generally fussed over her, a whole hour had gone by. She would have dragged things out even longer if Lily hadn't started to grizzle, no doubt hungry for her bottle.

Mentally bracing herself, Grace straightened her spine and carried her daughter downstairs and into the kitchen.

'You took your time,' Luca said from his seat at the table. He had removed his shirt. A short, rotund man was tending his shoulder, his bald head bowed in concentration. With a snap she recognised him as Giancarlo Brescia, the Mastrangelo family doctor. His presence should not be a surprise. Luca rarely travelled anywhere without him. People who lived by the sword and all that.

'I'm surprised you didn't send one of your goons up to keep watch,' she retorted, averting her eyes.

She didn't know what she found the most disturbing: his naked torso or the bloodstains marring his smooth skin. Some had matted into the swirls of black hair covering his chest. Dimly she recalled the many happy hours lying in his arms, breathing in his musky scent, splaying her fingers through the silky hair. Once upon a time, it would have taken a crowbar to prise her away from him.

'Believe me, you are going nowhere,' he said, his voice like ice.

'That's what you think.'

He laughed. A more mirthless sound she did not think she had heard. 'Do you really think I will let you disappear again, now, when I know you have had my child?'

'Who said she was yours?'

An animalistic snarl flittered across his handsome features but he remained still, the needle penetrating his flesh making any movement on his part risky. 'Do you think I would not recognise my own blood?'

She shrugged with deliberate nonchalance and sidled past him to the fridge, keeping a tight hold of Lily. She caught sight of the bloodied bullet laid oh-so-casually on the table and winced. She winced again to see the doctor expertly sew Luca's olive skin back together.

Luca followed her gaze. His nostrils flared. 'It lodged in a bone. There shouldn't be any permanent damage.'

'That's good,' she said, blinking away her shock at the physical evidence of his wound. Thank God she hadn't eaten breakfast. It would likely have come back up. She needed to keep a level head. Needed to keep her control.

She could not let guilt eat at her, and as for compassion… what compassion did Luca ever show *his* victims?

Turning her back to him, she pulled a bottle of formula out of the fridge and popped it in the microwave. She took a deep breath and punched in the time needed. The microwave sprang to life.

'Sorry to disappoint you, but she's not yours.'

The silence that ensued felt incredibly loaded, almost as if her lie had sucked all the air from the room, making her chest tight and her lungs crave oxygen. She could feel the burn of his eyes piercing the back of her skull, sending prickles of tension racing across her skin.

The microwave pinged, startling her. Was it always so loud?

She removed the bottle and shook it.

Lily must have caught the scent of milk because she started to whimper again.

'Shh,' Grace whispered. 'You can have it in a minute. Mummy needs it to settle first.'

Finally, unable to bear the tension another second, she tossed a glance over her shoulder.

Luca's eyes were fixed on her, his face tight, his features a curious combination of fire and ice.

The doctor had finished stitching the wound together and was cleaning the blood off his shoulder.

Smothering another retch, she sucked in more air in an attempt to stabilise her queasy stomach.

'Is your conscience playing up?' Luca asked, raising a mocking brow.

'No.' She turned her face away, the heat from another lie stinging her cheeks.

'No? It should be.'

'If anyone should have a troubled conscience, it is *you*.' She snatched up the bottle. 'I'm going to the living room to feed my daughter. Shut the door behind you when you leave.'

Not bothering to look for his reaction, she strode out of the kitchen. In the small living room she turned the television on and settled on a squishy sofa.

Since Lily had been born, Grace had become addicted to daytime television. And evening television. And nighttime television. The trashier the programme, the better. Concentrating on anything with any depth had become impossible.

She switched the channel to one of those wonderful talk shows featuring a dysfunctional family spilling its dirty laundry to a braying audience and a patronising host, and the incongruity of the situation almost made her laugh.

She could imagine herself on that stage, trying to justify shooting her own husband. Trying to justify a lot of things. Like ignoring all the signs that the man she loved was nothing but a gangster.

But love had blinded her. Or should that be lust? A combination of both that should have overwhelmed her in its intensity had instead been embraced. Without a second thought, she'd opened her heart wide enough to allow Luca to step right inside and burrow deep into her soul.

She had graduated art school full of the wonder of all life had to offer. Together with her best friend Cara, they had travelled Europe, visiting many of the architectural wonders in the continent.

Sicily was magical. She had fallen in love with the island and its gregarious inhabitants. Its more nefarious history had only added to the romantic ideal she had conjured.

Cara, an outdoor lover, had dragged her along for a hike over the mountainous terrain close to Palermo. They had followed what they joked was the longest fence in the world, a fence that kept outsiders from properly appreciating the most beautiful vineyards in the whole of Europe. When they had come to a gap in the fence they had assumed—wrongly—that it gave them a right of way. As luck would have it, the gap had led into an open meadow with the most spectacular views either of them had been privileged to see. Cara had been aching to paint it, so they had opened their picnic blankets out and set up; Cara with her watercolours, Grace with her sketchbook and pencils.

She had barely made a scribble when a black Jeep tore up the hill and screeched to a stop beside them.

That was when she had met Luca.

He had got out of the Jeep and walked towards them, a gun in his hand.

She should have been terrified. He had been dressed all in black, and her mind had immediately gone into an overdrive of images of swooping vampires and flesh-eating ravens.

While Cara had sensibly turned into a gibbering wreck, Grace had been entranced. It was as if she had inadvertently stepped into a movie shoot and the head vampire had come out from his coffin to greet them.

Looking back, she could hardly credit that she had been so blasé about a man with a gun, but she hadn't felt the slightest shiver of physical danger. She'd been so naïve she had assumed *all* Sicilian men carried guns. Fool that she was, she'd thought it all somewhat romantic.

Inexplicable tears filled her eyes and she blinked them away, sniffing loudly, disturbing Lily, who was busy guzzling her milk. The poor little mite was unaware her happy little life had irrevocably changed.

Footsteps sounded down the hall, followed by the sound of the front door closing.

She held her daughter ever tighter. She would rather die than be parted from her.

Somehow she didn't think Luca had been the one to leave the house.

Her intuition was bang on the money.

He strode into the living room as if he had every right to be there. His chest was still bare; a large white bandage had been placed over the wound on his shoulder, his arm resting in a sling.

He made straight for the television and turned it off.

'I was watching that.'

His nostrils flared. Not taking his eyes off her, he reached into his back pocket and produced two passports.

Blood rushed to her head so quickly it made her dizzy. Her hold on Lily tightened as she watched him, chills crawling up her spine.

Slowly, he waved the passports at her before sliding them back into his pocket.

'Lily Elizabeth Mastrangelo.' His words were monotone yet utterly remorseless. 'Her date of birth puts her at twelve weeks old.'

He might be injured but he still exuded the latent danger she had once found so exciting.

Why did he have to loom over her so? At five feet eight Grace was taller than the average female but next to Luca she always felt tiny.

Why, oh, why had she not moved on sooner? She had got back into physical shape relatively quickly. Obviously if she was comparing her recovery with that of a supermodel who managed to get back into her itsy-bitsy knickers within days, then she had been a failure.

In reality she had been fit enough to move on a month ago.

So why had she dragged it out?

Where had this abnormal lethargy come from?

Why had she not run the moment she had been fit enough?

'How dare you go through my handbag?' she said, dredging the words from a throat so arid it hurt to speak.

His eyes flashed. 'I have every right. You stole my child from me.'

Somehow she managed to grind the words out. She would not let him win. Not without a fight. 'She is not your child. I had to name you as her father because we're married.'

'Yes, she is.'

How she longed to slap the arrogant certainty from him.

'You did not have the opportunity for an affair and, besides, you loved me. Our sex life was incredible.'

A deep flush curled inside her, scattered memories of being wrapped in his arms, naked, his hard strength…

'*Loved* being the operative word,' she said, a little more breathlessly than she would have liked. '*Loved*, as in past tense. Lily is not your child.'

She refused to acknowledge his mention of the *S* word. The nightmares of the past ten months had been too great for her libido to do anything but wave a white flag. The only ache had been in her heart. And only in the dark early hours, when the world slept, did her heart acknowledge the aching absence within it.

Luca came before her and dropped to his haunches. The movement caused a fleeting wince to contort his features. The twisting sensation in her belly tightened. Being incapacitated in any form was anathema to him. She could have shot him a dozen times and he would still have the same vital, energising presence.

'*Bella*,' he said in a voice that was far too silky for comfort, 'she has the Mastrangelo hair. And you were still married to me when you conceived her. I know for a fact you did not cheat on me…'

The tension cramping inside her suddenly exploded and she met his gaze with wild eyes. How stupid was she to think for a single second he would even contemplate Lily being someone else's? Luca was so insufferably arrogant the thought of his wife cheating would be as likely as the moon being made of Stilton.

And how stupid was she to have named him as the father on the birth certificate?

'It's a bit hard to have an affair when your own husband has a tracker in your phone to monitor all your movements, and assigns two bodyguards to chaperone every single movement and report on anything the tracker fails to pick up.'

Lily had finished her bottle. She stared up at Grace, startled to hear her mother's raised voice.

Luca's lips formed a tight white line. Still on his haunches, he tilted forward. 'So you admit she is mine? You admit you wilfully kept my daughter's existence a secret?'

Forcing her voice down to a lower, calmer tone so as not to distress Lily, Grace stared at him with all the venom she could muster, willing him to feel every syllable that came from her lips like a punch to the gut. 'Yes. I hid her existence from you, and do you know what? I would do it again. Lily deserves better than to know of the monster who created half her DNA. You might be the sperm donor but *I* am her mother. She does not need you. And neither do I.'

The poison in Grace's voice cut through him, as sharp as a dagger.

Luca had taken one look at Lily and known she was his.

He could not say where this certainty had come from but there been no shadow of doubt in his mind. She was his.

He was a father.

Now his detestable wife had admitted the truth, he should feel relief. Instead, a raging burn was working its way through his system, a burn he was struggling to contain.

He would never have imagined such poison being uttered from the lips of his wife, a woman who always saw the best in people and always looked for the humanity in the face of evil.

He had never imagined she would look at him as if he were the Antichrist itself.

His guts rolled as he watched her lift their child onto her shoulder and rub her back, her movements gentle and loving.

The pain in his shoulder was immense. Once they were safely in the air he would take the painkillers Giancarlo had tried to get him to consume. Taking them would likely dull his reactions. Right now he needed every wit about him.

Unable to look at Grace a second longer, he got to his feet. 'I'm giving you half an hour.'

'For what?' she asked tightly, rubbing her nose into their daughter's thick black hair.

'To pack. Anything not packed will be left behind.'

That hateful venom came back into her voice. 'I'm not going anywhere.'

'You think not?' On legs that felt heavier than usual, he paced the small room. Somehow she had managed to cram a treadmill, an exercise bike and a rowing machine inside the tight confines. No wonder she had lost all her baby weight. No one looking at her would guess she had recently given birth. This, from the woman who had once told him with a straight face that she was allergic to exercise. 'I am not giving you a choice.'

'There is always a choice.'

Abruptly he stopped pacing and stared at her, making no attempt to hide his loathing. 'This is how we are going to play it: In exactly thirty minutes we will leave this place and return to Sicily.'

He took a breath.

Little more than an hour ago, he had been unaware Lily existed, unaware he was a father. Her thin eyelids were shut, displaying thick black Mastrangelo eyelashes.

His chest constricted, memories of his early childhood suddenly flooding him. His first memories. Waking up one morning at the age of three to find his parents missing. He remembered Bettina, his favourite maid, who was often given the task of watching over him, being red with excitement. His mother had gone to hospital to have the baby. He could still feel the eager anticipation he had experienced at that moment. Even clearer in his mind was the memory of his parents arriving home with the baby, his mother's pale, tired joy, his father's beaming pride. They had sat Pepe in Luca's arms on the sofa, and taken pictures of the small brothers together. He had been full to bursting with happiness.

Lily was the image of the baby Pepe had been.

This was his daughter.

And Grace had hidden her from him.

He looked at his wife. Her eyes were hollow, sunken, as if she hadn't slept for ten months. He was glad. Her guilt should not have allowed her any sleep.

'You call me a monster,' he continued, dropping his voice so as not to disturb the sleeping child. 'Yet I am not the one who vanished without a letter of goodbye. I'm not the one who decided her child would be better off without a father and conspired to keep me out of her life. And you have the nerve to call *me* a monster?'

Her clenched jaw loosened but her eyes remained unblinking as she said, 'I would do it again. In a heartbeat.'

Blood rushed straight to his forehead, colouring his thoughts, making his skin hot to the touch.

She had not the slightest remorse, not for anything. He could punish her, severely. He could snatch Lily from her arms and banish her from their lives and she wouldn't be able to do a single thing about it.

He could. But he wouldn't.

Luca had loved his parents equally but it had been his mother to whom he had gone with his cut knees and scrapes, his mother who had kissed his bruises better, his mother for whom a thousand hugs would never be considered enough.

Grace loved Lily. And Lily loved Grace. Already the bond between them was strong. It would take a heart of stone to break that bond.

Children needed their mothers and he refused to punish Lily for her mother's sins.

No, Grace's punishment would be of a different nature.

Blackness gripping his chest in a vice, he stalked towards her and bent over to speak in her ear. He could smell her fear through the clean scent of her skin and it gladdened him. He *wanted* her to fear him. He wanted her to curse the day she ever set foot in Sicily.

'You will never have the chance to take her away from me again. Lily belongs in Sicily with her family. You should consider yourself lucky I believe babies thrive better with their mothers or I would walk away with her right now and leave you behind to rot.' He paused before adding, deliberately, 'I would do it in a heartbeat.'

* * *

Grace closed her eyes tightly and clamped her lips together, trying desperately hard not to breathe. Luca's breath was hot against her ear, blowing like a whisper inside her. Tiny, tingling darts jumped across her skin, fizzing down her neck and spreading like a wave; responses that terrified her with their familiarity.

Her lungs refused to cooperate any longer and she expelled stale air, inhaling sweet clean oxygen within which she caught a faint trace of an unfamiliar cologne.

She forced her features to remain still, forced her chest to breathe in an orderly fashion. But she had no control over her heart. It jumped at the first inhalation and then pounded painfully beneath her ribs, agitating her nauseated stomach.

Luca wore one scent. He was not a man prone to vanity. Changing his cologne was not a triviality that would come on his radar.

She blinked the thought away. His mouth was still at her ear.

'You see, *bella*, you do have a choice,' he said, speaking in the same low, menacing tone. 'All I want is my daughter. Her well-being is all that matters to me. You can choose to stay in this cheap cottage, alone, or you can choose to return to Sicily with me and Lily, as a family.'

'I will *never* be part of your family again,' she said with as much vehemence as she could muster. 'I will never share your bed…'

He interrupted her with a cynical laugh. 'Let me put your mind at ease on that score. You have borne me a child. I have no need or desire to share a bed with you again. No, I will take a mistress for my physical needs. *You* will become a good Sicilian wife. You will be obedient and defer to my wishes in all things. That is the price you must pay if you wish to remain a part of Lily's life. And you will endure it with the grace that should be your namesake.'

'I hate you.'

He laughed again, a repulsive sound completely at odds with the deep, rip-roaring laughs she remembered. 'Believe me, you could not possibly hate me more than I hate you. You stole my child from me and, as you know, I am not a man who forgives people who act against me. But I am not a cruel man—if I were, I would take Lily and leave you behind without a second thought. Just as you would do to me.'

All she could do was stare at him, her heart, her pulses, her blood all pumping so hard her body trembled with the force.

He straightened to a stand, keeping his eyes locked on her. 'The *choice* is yours. Come to Sicily with me and Lily, or stay behind. But know this—if you stay, you will never see Lily again. If you come with us and then decide to leave, you will never see Lily again. If you come with us and I feel your behaviour is not befitting the role of a good Sicilian wife and mother, I will personally escort you off the estate and—'

'And I will never see Lily again,' she supplied for him dully.

He flashed his white teeth at her and inclined his head. 'So, we have an understanding. Now it is time for you to make up your mind. What is your *choice* to be?'

CHAPTER THREE

GRACE DID NOT think she had ever felt as nauseous as she did when the reinforced four-by-four came to a stop before the imposing electric gates. Two on-duty armed guards nodded at them respectfully as they drove through and into the Mastrangelo estate.

As they travelled along the smooth drive, cutting through rolling vineyards and verdant olive groves, the familiar scent of Sicilian nature at its crispest pervaded the air, flooding her with bittersweet memories.

After the freezing climate of Cornwall, a part of the UK that tended to have mild winters but was suffering from a particularly acute cold spell, the freshness of Sicily in December was a sharp contrast. The sun had yet to set, the brilliant cobalt sky unmarred by a single cloud. Her thick winter coat lay sprawled across her lap, her jumper warmth enough.

She turned her mind to her mobile phone and silently cursed.

She cursed the heavy snowstorm that had engulfed the south-west of England the previous week and made the roads so treacherous. If Lily hadn't needed to attend the local doctor's surgery for her three-month inoculation, she would never have attempted the journey. But she had. For safety's sake she had recharged the phone she had bought in Frankfurt for emergencies, and taken it with her on the hazardous bus journey, not dreaming that to do so would set in motion the wheels enabling Luca to find her. She had switched it back off the minute she returned home to her rented cottage.

She cursed that she hadn't dumped the stupid phone the moment she ended her brief calls to her mother and Cara all those months ago. She'd been in Amsterdam, waiting to catch a flight to Portugal. She'd reasoned that if Luca could trace the calls then good luck to him tracking her down at Schiphol Airport. She'd called her mum's landline but Cara only had a mobile phone. To play safe, she had advised Cara to destroy it. To play even safer, upon landing in Portugal she had hired a car and driven to Spain.

What she couldn't curse was using the phone in the first place. Her mum and Cara would have been the first people Luca contacted about her disappearance. After two weeks on the run and no contact, the guilt had been crippling her.

She looked at him now, sitting in the front passenger seat, his head turned to the side by the window. Such was his stillness she wondered if he had fallen asleep, dismissing the thought almost immediately. He had power-napped on the jet back home but his naps always evoked images of a guard dog sleeping with one ear up. He would not properly relax until he was safe inside his home.

As much as she hated him and everything he represented, Grace cursed herself too. The more she thought about the past wasted month, time she should have used moving herself and Lily to a remote Greek island as she had intended, the more she wanted to give herself a good slap.

She had watched her fill of gangster and mobster films in the ten months since fleeing Sicily, had read everything she could get her hands on about them too. *Know your enemy* had become her mantra. She had known the second

Luca found her he would not hesitate to have her dragged back to Sicily. As she had learned, it was the way of his world, where women were little more than possessions.

Which again begged the question, why? Why did she not move on when she had known the longer she stayed, the greater the trail she would be creating for him to find her? Even using Lily's inoculations as an excuse was no good—she'd had over a week since then to get her act together.

After a couple of miles they reached a larger wrought-iron gate, this one with guard shelters either side, both of which had monitors connecting to the larger security station in one of the estate cottages. From this point onwards, the ground was alarmed. Anyone who stepped onto the land triggered it, the boffins in the cottage using their technology to zoom onto the intruder. In all the time she had lived there the system had only been activated by large animals.

The head of security, Paolo, came out of the left shelter to greet Luca, tipping his cap as they exchanged a few words. When he spotted Grace in the back he nodded respectfully before returning to his station.

So he hadn't lost his job. She could not begin to describe her relief. As the person in charge of all security on the estate, losing the boss's wife was definitely on the 'do not do' list.

She leaned forward and rested a hand on the shoulder of Luca's seat. 'Thank you for letting Paolo stay in his job,' she said quietly.

He turned his head. 'If you mean the fact you were able to waltz out of the estate without an escort, then rest assured, I never blamed him for that.'

'I didn't waltz. I walked.' She had walked through acres and acres of vineyards and miles of arable land until she had found the field she was looking for. It was the same field she had inadvertently trespassed onto with Cara the day she first met Luca. The broken section of fence they had originally slipped through had long been mended. It took little effort to climb over it. It had felt prophetic, like coming full circle.

'I saw the footage. You looked as if you were going on an early-evening stroll. There was nothing in your demeanour to suggest you had no intention of returning. I give you credit, *bella*. You are a wonderful actress.'

Her coolness had been external only. As soon as she was off Mastrangelo land and no longer subject to scrutiny from the multitude of spying cameras, she had dumped the tracker-installed phone Luca had given her into a hedge and run, all the way to the nearest town. From Lebbrossi, she had taken a taxi to Palermo and caught the first flight off the island. That the first flight had been to Germany had been neither here nor there. If anything, it had done her a favour. It had made Luca's job of tracking her down difficult from the outset.

The drive veered to the right. As the four-by-four turned with it onto the straight she caught her first glimpse of the pink sandstone converted monastery. The late-afternoon sun beamed down, bathing it in a pool of warm light, setting off the brilliance of the simple architecture.

They drove through an arched entrance and into the courtyard, which the monastery wrapped around in a square.

No sooner had they stopped when the heavy oak front door flew open and a petite, raven-haired woman appeared.

Donatella. Luca's mother.

Throughout the journey back to Sicily, Grace had thought with varying degrees of emotion about her mother-in-law.

Donatella had never conformed to the stereotype of the traditional fire-breathing monster-in-law. If a little distant, she had treated Grace with nothing but courtesy and respect. All the same, Grace had never been that comfortable in her company, had always felt if Donatella had been able to choose a wife for her son, she would have chosen someone with traditional Sicilian values. The kind of woman Luca had sworn he never wanted her to be because he loved her exactly as she was. The type of woman he now wanted her to become.

She had no idea what kind of welcome she could expect from her.

Impeccably dressed as always in a smart skirt, blouse and elegant scarf, Donatella stepped into the courtyard.

Luca undid his seat belt before turning to face Grace. 'Remember my warning, *bella*. Now would be a good time to start channelling your inner Sicilian wife.'

Grace clenched her teeth together and glared at him.

With a flare of his nostrils he turned back and exited the car.

Her husband did not make empty promises. If she didn't live up to his expectations she would be torn from Lily's life without preamble or ceremony, and without any hope of appeal.

The situation was hopeless.

She hadn't called the police for assistance in England because they would have arrested her for possession of an illegal firearm, grievous bodily harm and God knew what other charges.

She could forget about assistance here in Sicily. This was Luca's territory and all the important people were in his pocket.

Grace tried to open her door but the child lock had been activated.

She crossed her arms and pursed her lips together.

As Luca and his mother conversed, both kept darting glances at the car. No guesses what they were talking about.

Taking a deep, steadying breath, she gazed down at Lily, who was fast asleep in the baby seat next to her. The poor thing was worn out, having spent the entire flight screaming, her ears no doubt affected by the air pressure. Grace had wanted to wail along with her. At that moment she would love nothing more than a chance to open her lungs and scream every ounce of frustration out of her.

Luca had defeated her. Despite all her efforts, he had won and now, unless she thought of an escape route, she was consigned to live in this medieval prison for the next eighteen years.

'I'll think of a way to get us out of here,' she promised quietly, rubbing a finger over Lily's tiny hand. 'And this time we'll go somewhere he'll never find us.' Outer Mongolia sounded nice.

His conversation over, Luca walked back to the car, opened her door, then strolled round and opened the door on Lily's side.

'I'll get her out,' she said, unclipping the seat belt.

His eyes were cool. 'I will.'

'You've only got one arm.'

'But I still have all my faculties.' He had the baby seat out before Grace had shut her door.

He carried the seat over to his mother, whose hands flew to her cheeks, a purr of pleasure escaping from her throat.

Grace could hardly bear to look. Donatella took the baby seat from him and carried her granddaughter inside.

Luca reached the front door and paused, staring at Grace impassively. 'Are you coming in or do you plan to spend the evening outside?'

Nodding sharply, she clutched Lily's baby bag to her and followed him inside.

It had been only ten months since she had last been in the converted monastery but as she took in the surroundings it felt as if she had been away for a lifetime.

With an enormous sense of déjà vu twisting in her stomach, she walked a step behind him down the wide main corridor, her boots crunching on the redbrick floor.

Luca was about to step into the large family room, one of the only communal rooms in the entire building, when he came to an abrupt stop. Tension emanating from him, he rolled his head back to stare at the ceiling before taking a long, deep breath. He swallowed. 'I have things to do.'

She caught a flash of eyes that burned before he turned and walked away.

For the beat of a moment, her lips parted to call him back. Being alone with his mother for the first time since running away from her son was infinitely more frightening than handling his gorilla-like lackeys.

Steeling herself, she stepped over the threshold.

All the decoration, paintings, furnishings…everything was exactly as she remembered it. As if time had stood still.

But of course, time had not stood still. Her own life had simply accelerated. She had lived a decade in less than a year.

The first time she had been in this room she'd been on top of the world, the happiest woman in existence. At the time she could never have foreseen that the beautiful walls would start to suffocate her. She certainly could not have foretold that the man she would marry would change with such speed, and that the gun she assumed he carried around for personal protection would take on a completely different meaning.

And now she was little more than his prisoner.

Donatella had removed Lily from her car seat and was

cradling her, a look of pure bliss on her perfectly made-up face.

Lily's eyes were open. If she was perturbed to be held in the arms of a stranger, she made no show of it.

Donatella's shrewd eyes flickered to Grace. 'She is beautiful.'

'Thank you.'

'And Lily; such a beautiful name.'

'Thank you,' she repeated, wondering if there had been a more excruciating, incongruous experience in the history of the world.

Luca's warning played over and over in her mind. Under no circumstances could she intimate she was there for any reason other than devotion. But it would help if she knew exactly what he had told his mother about her sudden reappearance in their lives and about the fact of Lily.

'It's getting late. I need to get Lily settled and into bed,' Grace said, not wanting to be stuck in an interrogation that was surely forthcoming and for which she didn't know the correct answers.

Her mother-in-law's eyes flashed before the lines around her mouth softened. 'Please, Grace, let me enjoy my first grandchild for a little longer. I have only just learned of her existence.'

A big stab of guilt twisted in her stomach. Reluctantly, she nodded. 'How about if I go and get our stuff unpacked and then come back for her?'

Donatella's grateful smile twisted the guilt a little more. 'That sounds perfect.'

Traipsing back up the corridor, Grace opened the door that led into the wing she had shared with Luca and took another step into the past.

This time all traces of the past really had been eradicated.

The only familiar item was a large family portrait on the wall, the last photo of the Mastrangelos taken before Pietro, Luca's father, had so tragically died. It had been taken at Luca's graduation. The pride shining on Pietro Mastrangelo's face was palpable. And who, she reflected, would not be proud of such a family? There was Luca, the eldest son, whose serious expression was countered by the amusement in his eyes. Next to him was Pepe, Luca's younger brother, whose air of mischief was not countered by anything. Then there was the composed, elegant Donatella. There was no pride on her face. Donatella radiated serenity. These men were her pride.

A mere two months after the picture had been taken, Pietro had died of a heart attack. The mantle of head-of-family had passed to his eldest son, Luca, a role he had now held for sixteen years.

Slowly she walked through the reception room and began opening the doors of all the rooms that made up their quarters. The vivid colours and delicate murals she had painted in each of the rooms had been painted over in drab, muted tones; the furniture they had chosen together replaced with bland, masculine replicas.

It was not until she opened the door to the master bedroom that her throat closed.

The walls she had spent literally scores of hours painting to create an erotic woodland, filled with beautiful cupids and lovers entwined, had been painted over. The walls she had been so proud of and conceived with such love and hope were now covered in a drab cream. They might never have existed.

Out of everything that had happened that day, this was the one thing that brought her closest to tears.

'You appear shocked.'

She hadn't heard Luca approach.

Her chest rose and she blinked rapidly, fighting the burn in her eyes before turning to face him. 'Not shocked,' she lied. 'More surprised.'

'You are surprised I would paint over the reminders of you?'

She went to tuck her hair behind her ear, an old habit she still couldn't break even though her hair had been cropped for months.

'I had no wish to sleep surrounded by lovers when my own wife had run away.'

'So you didn't change it because your new lover didn't approve?' Where that question came from, she was not quite sure, but the scent of his new cologne had wafted back under her nose.

Had he found a lover who had bought him this new scent?

Had this lover lain in his arms, in this very room, happy to drift into sleep with this scent imprinting on *her* senses?

Her belly churned at the images playing in her head.

Luca's eyes narrowed. 'I do not think you are in a position to ask me anything like that.'

She shrugged to display fake nonchalance at the subject. 'I couldn't care less who you've been screwing. As far as I'm concerned, the day I left we both became free agents.'

A large, warm hand reached out and cupped her shoulder. Even with one arm out of order, he trapped her against the wall with such efficiency she had no time to think, let alone resist. 'I do hope you're not implying that you've been with other men since you left me?'

'It would be none of your business if I had. Now let go of me.' Apart from his hand, none of his body touched her. But she could feel him. That heat that radiated from him; she could feel it. It warmed her, penetrating her skin, heating her veins. The way it always had.

The moment she had met him she had experienced the most incredible charge. It was as if she had been hit by a bolt of lightning. Whenever she was with him the charge would glow red-hot. While their marriage deteriorated, the bedroom had remained the one area in which they remained wholly compatible.

In all the time they had been apart she had not thought about sex. Not once. Protecting herself and her baby had consumed her. In the cold of night she had missed sleeping next to his warm, solid presence, but the actual sex was something she never thought about. Never allowed herself to think about. Assumed it had all been extinguished.

She couldn't breathe.

The extinguished charge that had flickered as if awakening from a deep sleep since he broke into her house came roaring back to life, and for the maddest of moments she longed to be taken into his arms, feel the firm warmth of his lips upon hers and his body harden…

'It is my business,' he contradicted silkily, his face square in front of her, forcing her to look into the fire spitting from his eyes. 'You are still my wife and Lily is my daughter. I have a right to know if you have allowed another man to act as her father.'

His breath was hot on her face, all her senses responding like a sweet-deprived child handed a bag of chocolate.

She twisted her head to the side. How she wished she could tell him tales of scores of lovers she had enjoyed in their time apart. 'There hasn't been anyone else.'

'Good.' He traced a finger down her turned cheek. 'And so there is no room for doubt, know that if you screw another man I will throw you onto the street. You won't even have time to forget to write a note.'

CHAPTER FOUR

LUCA RELEASED HIS hold and took a step back, taking in Grace's heightened colour and the indignation ringing out from her eyes.

He had touched her soft cheek, inhaled her clean, feminine scent, and for the shortest of moments he had experienced a softening in his chest and a hardening in his groin.

Of all the women in all the world, what the hell had possessed him to marry this one? At that moment, he could not recall a single rational reason.

Fantastic sex and an unwillingness to let her out of his sight had been the primary reasons. If he had slowed down a little and comprehended that marrying a free-thinking artist might not be compatible to his way of life, he would surely have kept their relationship to that of lovers. His mother and brother had both warned him of the dangers. He had curtly told them to mind their own business.

He had been smitten. He had fallen head over heels in love, unable to imagine his life without her. Only when she had his ring on her finger had he been able to relax and thank God for bringing her to him. But only after they had signed on the dotted line did he fully comprehend how difficult it would be keeping safe a woman who refused his protection and refused to take his entreaties to be careful seriously.

Well, now she would be given no choice. All that mattered was the well-being of his daughter, and Grace would damn well have to put up with the rules he laid down.

Her breaths were coming in short, shallow bursts. Her eyes were fixed on him, an odd combination of hate and desire pouring out of them. He understood the combination.

Once he had loved her.

Now he despised her.

And after everything she had done, he still desired her.

His sling dug into his collarbone and he welcomed the distraction it provided. She was like poison, an intoxication that had embedded into his bloodstream for which an antidote had yet to be found. 'Would you like me to tell you something amusing?'

'Not particularly.'

'You will like this. You see, *bella*, my search for you was just that—a search. All I wanted was to hear in your own words the reason you left me. You took the coward's way out and I wanted an explanation. Nothing more. I would have left you alone to live your life.'

'Yeah, right,' she stated flatly.

'Yes, that is right.' He shook his head with more savagery than intended. 'You should have told me about the pregnancy. I am a reasonable man. We could have come to an agreement.'

'You? Reasonable? The only agreement would have been on your terms and would have meant me moving back to Sicily.'

'If that is what you choose to believe then go ahead. As you did not take that route the outcome is something you will never know.' He would not give her the satisfaction of knowing she was right but not for the reasons she thought. He'd imagined that all he'd need was five minutes alone with her before she begged to return to Sicily, to return to him. Any other outcome had been incomprehensible.

Such foolish imaginings.

Not that it mattered. Grace was his wife. She belonged to him.

He turned to the door, ready to open it and escort her out of the room. This was all too much. It hurt to even look at her.

Grace spotted a faint glimmer of opportunity. 'Let me and Lily go,' she blurted out before he could open the door. 'If you never intended to bring me home, why put either of us through this?'

Luca had learned he was a father only that morning, she reasoned. Shock could lead to irrational actions, as she knew well. It had been the shock of seeing that poor man's battered face and body, and the *fear* on his face when he recognised her. That, along with the aftershocks of her and Luca's ferocious argument still reverberating through her, had provided the spur she needed to leave. She had spent the drive back from her shopping trip mute with shock. Her brain frozen, she had walked into the bedroom she shared with the man she loved. She had gazed at the cherubs and lovers on the walls and had felt nothing. All the happiness and feeling had been sucked out of her.

The man she had married with such hope and such all-encompassing love was nothing but a criminal. And a dangerous one at that. Whether he'd been a criminal or not when they'd first married had been moot. It made no difference to the man he had become.

'It won't be any good for Lily,' she continued, resolve spurring her on. 'Can you imagine how awful it will be for her growing up knowing her parents hate each other?

Because she will feel it. She will. Children are like emotional sponges.'

'Lily will not suffer because I will not allow it,' he bit back. 'And if you want to remain in her life then you will not allow it either. If I think at any time that you are trying to poison her against me, you will be gone. Now, if you will excuse me, it has been a long day and I would like to shower. You have been put in the blue room.'

Yanking the door open, he held it for her. She couldn't help notice the wince of pain he gave and the tight, queasy feeling in her belly rippled.

She stalked past, flinching when he slammed it shut behind her. Only when she was safely in her new room did she start to shake.

She sank onto the bed and held Lily's bag to her chest, blinking rapidly, trying to catch her thoughts.

The blue room was exactly as it had been when she left. Blue. Blue walls, blue curtains, blue furnishings...even the en suite was the blasted colour. It was the one room of their wing she had never got around to personalising. It had been next on her to-do list, before the discovery of the truth had sent her fleeing.

She hated this room, had deliberately left it until last because she had known this room above all others would give her the greatest fulfilment.

Unzipping a compartment of the bag, she pulled out her fated phone. If there was one silver lining to this imprisonment it was that she could now speak to her mum and Cara. It would be the first time she had spoken to either of them in ten months.

It had been safer all round that no one knew where she was hiding, something she had found especially hard in England. She had known moving to Cornwall was pushing her luck to its limit, but the closer she had come to giving birth, the lonelier and more frightened she had become. There she was, about to go through the most terrifying, life-changing experience of her life and she had no one to share it with. Knowing her mother was only three hundred miles away had at least brought some comfort, but in all honesty her mum would have been a useless birth partner.

Billie Holden was an artist too—a sculptor—but reality rarely intruded in her life. Grace laughed sourly as she acknowledged it was a trait she had inherited—after all, hadn't she refused to allow reality to intrude on her love for Luca?

She remembered her call to Billie from Schiphol Airport with a smile. Typical of her mum, she'd been unfazed when Grace had explained the situation, merely relieved her only child was alive. Even when Grace had said she might not be able to contact her for a very long time, Billie had reacted with a cheery, 'Never mind, my darling, you're the best-equipped person I know to fend for yourself.' She'd probably envisaged Grace's situation as a great adventure rather than confront the reality of the situation.

Grace's childhood had been different from those of her friends. Her mother had treated her like a best friend rather than a daughter. Not for her rigid bedtimes or mealtimes—it was a rare day when Billie even remembered to cook a meal—or the relentless nagging all her friends received. Instead, Grace had been encouraged to embrace life and given all the freedom she desired. Her father was of the same mindset and every bit as much of a dreamer as her mum, but where Billie poured all her energy into her art, Graham devoted his to worthy causes in the developing world, disappearing for months, sometimes years, on end.

For all her parents' benign neglect, Grace had never doubted their love for her. It was just a different love from that which most other parents gave. And if there had been moments—many moments—when she had yearned to test them and ask how deep their love for her ran, she wouldn't swap them for anyone or change a single day of her childhood.

At least she could now make proper contact without worrying that Luca had tapped Billie's phone or could trace her IP address.

For better or for worse, she would no longer have to look over her shoulder. At least, not until she found a way to escape again.

Luca lay in his bed, listening as Lily's cries lessened. The door to the makeshift nursery opened and he heard soft footsteps go past his room.

He willed his eyes to shut but they refused, just as they had refused since he had come to bed five hours ago.

There was too much going on in his head to sleep. This was the first time he had been alone with his thoughts since he had learned of Grace's location. Not even the sedatives in his painkillers could switch his brain off.

He had found her. After ten long months he had really found her. It had all happened so quickly the day held a dream-like quality to it. Or was it a nightmare?

He was a father. That was his daughter crying in the dark. That was his wife comforting her. She was here, back under his roof. Unwillingly back under his roof.

There were no words to describe the loathing he felt towards Grace, as if an angry nest of vipers were festering in his guts, stabbing their fangs into him.

Nothing would give him greater pleasure than to pack her stuff and tell her to leave, to get out and never come back. But he could not. Even after everything she had put him through, he retained enough rationality to know it would be Lily who would suffer the most.

No, Grace's punishment would be of an entirely different nature.

From now on, when they entertained guests or left the estate, she would damn well be deferential towards him. No longer would he tolerate having his business activities probed, his opinions contradicted or his word questioned. No longer would he tolerate a wife who neglected her appearance because her mind was too full of whatever she was currently creating on a canvas to run a brush through her hair or wear clothes that matched. No longer would he find these particular quirks endearing.

He'd never met anyone like her before: someone who saw all the colour the world had to offer. Before Grace, the women he'd dated had always been perfectly turned out with opinions that were in line with his own. They could have been identikit. Until Grace appeared, as if by magic, casting him under her spell, he'd never realised how boring he found them all, or how predictable his life had been.

He'd taken such pride in her talents and the freshness she'd brought to his life that the last thing he'd wanted to do was change her in any way.

He'd loved her exactly as she was.

Well, more fool him.

Grace would learn to be a proper Sicilian wife.

Sleep was not going to come any time soon. Throwing the sheets off, he climbed out of bed and pulled on his dressing gown, carefully navigating the sling.

All the lights were off.

Grace and Lily were nowhere to be found.

He opened every door in the wing, his chest tightening with every empty room.

He returned to Grace's room. Her suitcases lay on the floor, seemingly unpacked. Her toothbrush and toothpaste had been laid on the sink of the en suite, a bulging bag of toiletries placed on the cabinet.

Entering the adjoining room, he flipped on the light. His heart twisted at the empty cot. A pile of nappies and baby accessories he did not recognise had been neatly placed on the dresser.

Where the hell had they gone?

Just as he was debating waking the household and conducting a thorough search for them, Grace walked into the room, her dressing gown covering her tall, slender frame, carrying Lily and a bottle of formula.

Immediately she switched the light off but not before he caught the glare she directed at him.

She walked soundlessly past him and settled in the old rocking chair, curling her legs in a ball and placing the teat of the bottle in Lily's tiny mouth. 'I want her to go back to sleep after she's had this,' she whispered, nodding at the light switch.

'Where have you been?' he asked, adopting an identical whisper.

'In the kitchen warming the bottle up.'

The kitchen was on the other side of the monastery. In the early hours of winter it was always freezing down there. 'Why didn't you get a member of staff to do it for you?'

Even in the dusky light he could clearly identify the look of disdain that crossed her face. 'Apart from your security guards, everyone's asleep.'

'Does she always wake so early?' It was five a.m.

She nodded. 'If I'm lucky she might go back down for another couple of hours. I had worried that after all the travelling she might have trouble settling, but she nodded off without any problems.'

'In future I will ensure someone is available to warm the milk for you.'

She rolled her eyes. 'I'll get a kettle and a jug brought up to my room.'

'That's what I pay the staff for.'

'Luca, I'm not going to argue with you about it. I'm not going to have someone else's sleep disrupted for the sake of a kettle and a jug.'

'I think you'll find you are already arguing with me about it.'

The whisper of a smile curved on her cheeks. 'No change there, then.'

Grace had always enjoyed sparring with him but it had always been done in a gentle, amused fashion. She was the only person, aside from his mother and brother, who did not automatically assume his word was on a par with God's. She challenged him, made him look at the world through a different prism. Where he saw things in black or white, she saw the varying shades of grey in between. It was one of the many things he'd loved about her: the context and sense she helped him make of the world.

Having taken over the running of the estate at the age of twenty-one, he'd been so focused on keeping the high standards set by his father and keeping his family safe from those who would snatch everything away from them, he'd never had the time to really think about *his* place in the world.

When, a year into Luca's marriage, Francesco Calvetti, an old childhood acquaintance whose family had been the Mastrangelos' bitter enemies, had suggested going into business together, it had seemed like perfect timing. Luca had already been toying with the idea. Both men were keen to establish themselves away from the long shadows cast over them by their respective fathers and equally keen to end a feud neither had wanted.

Being with Grace and the fresh perspective she had on

life had, for the first time, made him see that the life he had been living was the life expected of him. He was living in his father's footsteps. His own hopes and dreams had been suppressed for the good of the family. For duty.

It was time to strike out in his own name.

Yet, for all the context his wife had given his world, he failed to see the context or sense in why she had run away.

She thought he was a monster. She had wilfully kept their child a secret from him. Where was the context in that? So they'd had an argument? All couples rowed. One proper argument was not good enough reason to rip a marriage apart.

A lump formed in his chest. He swallowed hard to dislodge it. 'Did you find everything you need in the nursery?'

'Pretty much. Thank you. And thank you for putting me next to her.' She adjusted her hold on Lily and looked back at him. The rising sunlight was slowly dispersing the dusky grey, her features becoming clearer by the passing minute. 'I admit, when you said I was to have the blue room, I thought it was deliberate because you knew how much I hated it. It took a while for me to remember it adjoined another room.'

'She is sleeping in my old cot,' he said. 'My mother got the staff to take it out of hibernation.'

'I did wonder.'

He should leave; return to *his* room. Instead he found his eyes transfixed on the feeding baby. *His* feeding baby. *Their* feeding baby. A child he and Grace had created together.

A part of him longed to reach over and touch her, to stroke his baby's face, to hold her to his chest and feel her warmth on his skin, to smell that sweet, innocent scent.

They looked so perfect together. Even Grace could not create a more beautiful picture.

A spike cut through his heart, piercing him, a pain a

thousand times stronger than the ache in his shoulder. It took all his strength not to sway with its force.

And there was another ache too, a much baser ache that should not exist for her, not any more.

His sex drive had always been high but Grace was the only woman who had been able to turn him to lava with nothing more than a seductive smile or the flash of a shoulder. To his body, there was no more desirable a woman. Even the curve of her ankle was erotic.

There were times when he would swear she was a sorceress. How else could he explain the hold she had over him, the unquenchable yet ultimately poisonous desire that lived in his blood? Why else had he not grabbed his freedom when he'd had the chance, as any other red-blooded Sicilian man would have done?

But he'd had no time for such pursuits. What with running the estate and his other, newer, business interests, there had been no time for any kind of affair. On top of all that, the main focus of his energies had been spent on tracing Grace. Sex had never crossed his mind.

To discover his libido had reawoken because of her and that he could still respond when she wore nothing but a tatty old dressing gown sickened him. That his fingers ached to lean over and trace the delicate line of her neck, that his lips tingled to press against her…

He dragged his gaze upwards and found her staring at him, the same pained yearning mirroring back at him, her angular cheeks heightened with colour. Then her eyelids snapped a blink and she turned her face away.

Clenching his hands into fists, Luca looked to the door and willed his thundering heart to slow.

The sooner he found himself a lover, the sooner he could be released from the sexual hold she still held on him.

The sooner he stopped thinking about making love to his wife, the better.

'Write a list of everything you need for you and Lily, and I'll get someone to get it for you tomorrow.'

Closing the door softly behind him, he went back to his room and fired up his laptop.

There was no way he would be able to get any sleep now.

Work would be his salve, as it had been since Grace disappeared. Work would help focus his attention on the matters that truly deserved it, not the deceptive, heartless bitch he had been foolish enough to marry.

As Grace tiptoed back into her bedroom from the adjoining nursery there was a rap on the door.

She hurried over and yanked it open, her fingers already flying to her lips.

'Shh,' she whispered. 'I've only just got her down for a nap.'

'Here's your passport,' Luca said without any preamble, extending it to her, making no move to step over the threshold.

Snatching it from his hand, she flipped through it. 'I did wonder if you would give it back to me.'

'Why would I want to keep it?' he said, his top lip curving. 'You are free to leave whenever you like.'

'And Lily's passport?'

'I will be keeping that.'

She expected nothing less. 'I suppose it's pointless asking where, exactly, you will be keeping it?'

'You presume correctly. Now give me your phone.'

'I'm surprised you didn't take it from me yesterday.' Turning her back to him, she grabbed it off her bedside table where it was charging.

'Today will suffice.'

She passed it to him. 'I take it you're going to put a tracker in it.'

'You're getting good at this—you assume correctly. If you need to make a call before I get it back to you, use the landline.'

How she hated the coldness of his tone. And how she hated that she hated it.

'I'll do that,' she said with a brittle smile. As he had still not stepped over the threshold she took great delight in shutting the door, quietly, in his face.

The smile dropped. She leaned back against the closed door and crossed her hands over her racing heart.

Her phone was returned that afternoon by one of the maids. She took it from her gingerly and threw it onto the bed. It felt tainted. The first chance she got, she would buy herself a new pay-as-you-go one.

Purchasing another phone turned out to be trickier than anticipated.

When she felt ready to take Lily on a Sicilian shopping trip two days later, a Mercedes was brought out for her. Three heavies were sitting in it.

The number of her personal 'guards' had been increased.

Pushing Lily around Palermo, her gorillas surrounding her, she knew she was onto a lost cause.

Their presence only served to remind her of what she had hated most about her marriage. Before she had opened her eyes to her husband's true nature, the biggest blot on the marital landscape had been the lack of privacy. Sure, on the estate she could come and go as she pleased, but she had always been aware of hidden cameras, supposedly there for all the Mastrangelos' protection, watching her every move on the grounds. Outside the estate, she was under constant armed guard. She couldn't even pop off to buy a paintbrush without one of Luca's gorillas accompanying her.

She had hated it.

She still hated it, loathed the thought of her daughter growing up in an environment where freedom meant nothing.

Freedom was precious. It was unrealistic and dangerous to expect Lily to have the same levels of freedom she had enjoyed, but, unless she found an escape route, her daughter would never experience what it meant to be a proper, regular child. She would never be able to explore and get into mischief without her parents knowing her every move. She would always be in her father's eyeline no matter where he was.

All the material advantages Lily would have being a Mastrangelo would be cancelled out by the disadvantages. And that was without considering what it would be like growing up with a father who was a dangerous gangster.

While Grace didn't believe for a second that Luca would lay a finger on either of them, his rages, which in the last six months or so of their marriage had become more frequent, could be terrifying. Especially for a child. She never wanted her daughter to witness that.

When she returned to the monastery, she carried Lily to the private front door of their wing. Before she could unlock it, Donatella materialised. 'I thought you would want to know that Pepe will be returning tomorrow,' she said, referring to Luca's younger brother who had his own, rarely used, separate wing in the monastery. Pepe was the family firebrand, a playboy rebel without any discernible cause. Yet, despite his outward rebelliousness, he was fiercely loyal to his family.

Grace was not looking forward to his return. Pepe would know the truth of what had gone on between her and Luca.

The last time she had seen him, Pepe and Luca had had a massive argument. She still had no idea what the row had been about but it had been heated enough for her to worry that one of them would get hurt. It still made her blood freeze whenever she recalled questioning Luca about it afterwards and their own subsequent row.

'Thanks for the warning.' She placed the key in the lock and as she turned it Donatella placed a bony hand on her arm.

'Why did you return?'

Grace eyed her warily. There was little point in saying it was because of love. The atmosphere between her and Luca was so cold and yet somehow so charged, the entire household had to be aware things were not right between them. 'What has Luca told you?'

'Luca does not confide with me. All he has said is that he found you and you agreed to try again. He still has not told me why you left to begin with, or what happened to his shoulder.'

Grace blanched. She shook her head, trying to clear the fog that clouded it every time she thought of it. She could still smell the gun smoke.

She could also see the poor beaten man whose eyes had widened with terror when he recognised her as Luca's wife.

'I'm sorry, but it's for Luca to tell you what happened.'

Donatella studied her for a moment before digging into her pocket and producing a key.

Grace stared at it.

'It's the key for your studio,' Donatella said, passing it to her. A shadow crossed her face. 'Luca refused to let anyone in there. He said it was yours until you returned, even if you only came back to collect your belongings.'

'He said that?'

A sliver of ice shot out of her mother-in-law's eyes. 'I am

not a stupid woman. I can tell you do not wish to be here. But you *are* here even if the circumstances are not what you or my son would wish.'

With those enigmatic words, Donatella walked off.

CHAPTER FIVE

IT TOOK ANOTHER two days before Grace gave in. Leaving Lily with Donatella, who was delighted to be granted her first official babysitting duty, she headed through the thick forest that surrounded the monastery to her cottage.

Her cottage. Given to her by Luca on their wedding day.

She could still recall her excitement when she'd first walked inside and seen the lengths he had gone to to make it into a proper studio for her. The walls of the ground floor had been knocked down to make one enormous room, and painted white to enhance the natural sunlight. Daylight-mimicking light bulbs had been installed for when the muse took her at night. There were easels to accommodate all different sizes of canvas, a hundred different brushes of varying sizes and hair and, best of all, he had bought every shade of paint from the specific brand she favoured. She had been in heaven.

She had not picked up a paintbrush or done anything as basic as a doodle since she had left. All her creative juices had died when she walked out of the estate.

Taking a deep breath, she turned the key and pushed the door open. Immediately she was hit with the trace of turpentine and oil paint, scents that had seeped into every crevice of the cottage.

At first glance it looked exactly as she had left it. The

canvas she had been working on was still on its easel, a fine layer of dust now covering it; her brushes all rammed into varying pots, her tubes of paint still scattered randomly across her workbench. Stacks of blank and completed canvases still lay in neat stacks; half-finished canvases she had left to dry before working on them again still lined the walls.

Someone had been in there during her absence. It was nothing specific she could put her finger on, more of a gut feeling.

Her stomach tying itself in knots, she climbed the open staircase to the first floor. The sense that someone had been there grew stronger, especially when she entered the bedroom. This was the room she had slept in whenever Luca was abroad or tied up with business until the early hours, something that had dramatically increased throughout the second year of their marriage. Although she'd missed him being around so much, she would take the opportunity to work through the witching hours without guilt and then flop into bed shattered.

One thing she had always been able to take heart from was that he would always join her if he was in Sicily. Wherever she slept, he would seek her out. Always. She would wake to find herself wrapped in his arms. Invariably, they would make love and she would tell herself that everything between them was fine.

She was certain she had left the bed unmade.

The bathroom was dusty but clean, relatively tidy, her toothbrush and other toiletries on display where she had left them. A quick peek in the laundry basket revealed the tatty jeans and paint-splattered jumper she had last worked in.

Her bittersweet trip down memory lane was interrupted when she heard the front door shut.

'Hello?' she called, hurrying to the stairs. About to step

down, she paused when she saw Luca leaning against the front door staring up at her.

'What do you want?' They were alone for the first time since he had found her. Now there was no Lily to temper the tone of her voice for, she made no attempt to hide her hostility.

The first thing she noticed was his lack of a sling. Dressed in black jeans and a light blue sweater, his arms folded across his broad chest, his jawline covered in dark stubble, he carried a definite air of menacing weariness.

'We've been invited to Francesco Calvetti's birthday party in Florence next Saturday,' he said without any preamble.

'Why's he holding it in Florence?' Francesco Calvetti was as big a gangster as her husband. It was only after Luca had invested in a couple of casinos and nightclubs with him that the cracks in their marriage had appeared and he had begun to change…

'He bought a hotel there. I've accepted the invitation for us.'

'It's far too short notice.'

'I wasn't asking your opinion on the matter. I was telling you.'

'And what about Lily?'

'I have spoken to my mother and she has agreed to care for her overnight.'

'Absolutely not.' No way was she going to leave her baby to attend *that* man's party.

'I have also seen the local priest about having Lily baptised,' he continued as if she hadn't spoken. 'I have booked her in for the first Sunday of the new year.'

'Well, that's telling me,' she said, stomping down the stairs. 'We can argue about the christening in a minute. I am not leaving Lily to attend a silly party.'

'It is not a silly party. It is an important event that you will attend as my devoted wife.'

The way his eyes burned into her left Grace with no doubt as to the meaning laced in his words.

Devoted wife.

Luca might have abandoned the idea of displaying togetherness in front of his family but this did not extend to the wider world.

She would be expected to accompany him and act the docile, dutiful wife.

She would be expected to play the role of lover to a man she hated with every fibre of her being. The consequences of failure would be harsh. Banishment from her daughter's life.

'Am I at least allowed a say in the christening? Or is Lily's entire future to be decided by you?'

His nostrils flared. 'That all depends.'

'On what?'

'On whether your opinions concur with mine.'

'So that'll be never, then,' she threw at him bitterly.

'Consider yourself lucky to be here and able to voice an opinion,' he said, his tone a low, threatening timbre. 'It's a sight more than you gave me.'

'It's a sight more than you deserved,' she spat. 'Now, unless there's something else you want to tell me, you can leave.'

Luca clenched his fists by his sides at her defiance, at the folded arms crossed over the slender waist, her hair sprouting in all directions. Since they had returned, the red dye had faded, her natural honey blonde coming through.

He didn't know if he wanted to wrap his hands around her throat or kiss the defiance from her face.

She had been home for six days. In all that time he had

tried to block her from his mind but she was still there, festering in his psyche. He didn't want to exchange one solitary word more than was necessary with her. Simply looking at her deceitful face made his stomach clench.

'I am not yet ready to leave. You owe me some answers.'

Her striking features contorted into something feral. 'I don't owe you anything.'

Every sinew in his body tightened. When she turned her back on him and walked to her workbench, he had to fight the urge to wrench her round and force her to look at him.

'You damn well do. One minute you were there, the next you were gone. No letter, no phone call, nothing to let me know if you were dead or alive.'

She turned around, leaned against the bench and rolled her eyes. 'Steady on, Luca—you make it sound as if you were worried about me. Surely a heart is needed to feel worry?'

It was the dripping cynicism that did it for him. The sheer lack of remorse. The implication that her selfish, unrepentant behaviour was somehow *his* fault.

All the rage he had been smothering since he found her exploded out of him, consuming him in a fury that accelerated when he found his tongue to speak.

'Worried about you?' he said, his words coming out in a raging flow. 'Worried about you? I thought you were dead! Do you hear me? Dead! I imagined you lying cold on a verge. I pictured you cold in a mortuary. For two weeks I could not sleep for the nightmares. So no, I wasn't worried about you. It was *much* worse than that.'

For a moment he thought he caught a flicker of distress on her face before her now familiar insouciance replaced it. 'I apologise if I caused you any distress…'

Slam!

Without conscious thought, the desperate need to

purge the storm of emotions acted for him and he punched the wall.

'You haven't got a clue, have you?' he raged. 'I thought we were happy. When you went missing, I thought you'd been kidnapped but when I received no ransom I thought you had been killed. I called your mother, I called Cara—neither of them had heard from you. Or so they said. It never crossed my mind you would do something so wicked as to up and leave without a word.' He threw his arms out, ignoring the pain in his shoulder, ignoring the throb in his fist. 'You didn't just leave me, you left everything, all your work, all your clothes…'

In the midst of his fury he saw how white she had become, how she clung to her workbench as if she depended on it to keep her upright.

Taking a deep, ragged breath, he fought for control and forced his voice to adopt a modicum of calm. 'Two weeks after you went missing, your bank statement arrived. I opened it and found every euro had been transferred into a new account the same day you disappeared. Do you know how I felt then?'

Slowly, she shook her head.

'Elated. Suddenly there existed the possibility you were alive. Until then it hadn't even occurred to me to check the safe for your passport.' When he had discovered it missing, the relief had been so physical he had slumped to the floor and buried his head in his hands, sitting there for minutes that had felt like hours, his usually quick brain taking its time to process the implications. But once he had processed them…

He had dug up all her bank statements and read them in detail. Apart from the odd splurge on painting materials, Grace had hardly touched the allowance he gave her.

Over a two-year period she had accumulated more than two million euros.

Had she been planning her escape from the start?

Whatever the reason, his wife had saved enough money to start over.

From then, it had been a case of following the money trail. Luckily for him, money—his money—was able to lubricate the tightest of lips and within a day he had been in Frankfurt. Unluckily for him, he had been a week too late. She had already gone. It had taken another four months for him to find her latest location but he had been too late then too.

In the meantime, Pepe had come up trumps with Cara's phone, through which they'd determined what they had good reason to believe was Grace's number. That same number had remained inactive until barely a fortnight ago.

'You put me through hell,' he said flatly. 'I would have gladly traded my life for yours and you let me believe you were dead. Now tell me why I don't deserve some answers.'

'I was going to leave you a note,' she said. For the first time he detected a softening in her voice. 'But I couldn't risk you coming home early and finding it before I had a chance to leave Sicily. I knew you would never let me go.'

'What kind of a monster do you think I am?' he asked, throwing his arms back in the air. 'That argument we had before you disappeared? Was that the cause of it?'

'No! That row—as horrible as it was, I would have forgiven it in time…'

'So tell me! When, exactly, did I frighten you so much that you believed I would stop you doing anything?'

'That's just it! You never let me *do* anything.' She threw her own arms in the air. 'You promised I could exhibit my work in Palermo and it came to nothing—every time I found the perfect venue you found the perfect excuse to keep me from buying it. I wasn't allowed to drive my own car, I had to travel everywhere with armed guards—I couldn't even buy a box of tampons without one of your goons hovering over me. I would insist he stay outside the shop door but I couldn't be certain he didn't have his binoculars out spying on me, ready to report back to you.'

'My men were assigned for your own protection, not to spy on you,' he roared. 'They were there to keep you safe. This isn't England. You knew when you married me that you were marrying into—'

'I most certainly did not! I took you at face value. I thought *everyone* in Sicily carried guns for their personal protection. If I had so much as suspected the kind of monster you really were…' Her vicious tongue suddenly stopped, her eyes widening, fixing on his shoulder. 'Luca, you're bleeding.'

Sure enough, when he followed her line of sight down to his shoulder, a dark stain had appeared. Immediately he became aware of the accompanying ache.

Now he was aware of it, his knuckles throbbed too.

Grace stared for a moment longer, then turned and dragged a paint-splattered chair over to him. 'Sit down and take your top off,' she ordered in short, clipped tones. 'I'll get the first-aid kit.'

'Stop trying to change the subject,' he said. With all the bitterness and acrimony flying around, a sour taste had formed in his mouth. 'You were about to explain what you find so abhorrent about me.'

White-lipped, her jaw clenched, she sank to her knees in front of a small cabinet. 'You're hurt,' she said as she rummaged through it. 'My home truths won't mean a thing if you bleed to death. Let's sort your wound out first.'

Yes, he was hurt. Heartsick and nauseated with a chest

so tight it was difficult to draw breath. 'You are the last person I want tending to any of my injuries, now or ever.'

A small green bag with *first aid* written on it whipped over and landed by his feet.

'If you want to bleed to death like a stuck pig, be my guest. Or, if you want to be an adult about it, let me take a look at your wound.'

She stood before him, hands on hips, glaring at him. He had always known she had proper backbone but its strength had only become fully apparent since he found her.

An image flickered in his hammering brain of his wife facing off against their teenage daughter. Would Lily inherit her mother's independent streak? How often would he have to step in as peacemaker when they faced off to each other?

That was if they lasted that long. At the rate he and Grace were going they would be lucky to see the new year in without killing each other. He could feel the fury that resided in her as clearly as he could feel his own.

He inclined his head and then carefully removed his sweater and shirt.

With brisk efficiency, Grace picked up the first-aid kit and brought another chair over to sit opposite him.

She tilted her head and studied him. 'You've torn the stitches.' Unzipping the kit bag, she removed a square foil package and ripped it open with her teeth. 'Keep still.'

Her head bowed in concentration, she used the antiseptic wipe to clean the blood with her right hand, her left hand resting lightly on his thigh to steady herself.

His senses filled with the fragrance of her shampoo tickling his nose. The trace of turpentine that had become more elusive the longer she had been gone was there too, more pronounced than it had been in months.

Being back in her studio with her filled him with emotions he could not begin to comprehend.

How he had loved watching her paint, watching the deep concentration she applied to her art. She would cut out the world from inside her head so all that remained was her and the canvas that became an extension of herself. If he was home, he would bring his laptop to the studio and work while she painted. For the most part she would be oblivious to his presence, but every now and then she would turn her head and bestow him a beaming smile that left him in no doubt how happy she was to have him there with her.

Even before she disappeared he had missed those times, but the running of the casinos and nightclubs had taken him away from home more frequently than he would have liked, especially in the evenings.

'I like what you've done to your hair.'

She stilled and raised her eyes. 'I thought you would hate it.'

'Is that why you cut it so short? To spite me?'

'Partly. Mostly it was to make it harder for you or anyone searching to recognise me. Every time I moved on I would cut a little more off and change the colour.'

'It's just as well I found you when I did or you would have ended up looking like a Tibetan monk.'

She laughed, but it sounded forced. 'Yes. I might have ended up in a proper working monastery. You would never have found me then.'

'Probably not.' He expelled a breath. There was something incredibly soothing about the way she tended him, her fingers gentle and unrushed. He closed his eyes as he felt the now familiar hardening in his groin.

He did not want to want her.

He *shouldn't* want her.

But dear God he did.

'The bleeding's stopped,' she murmured. 'I'll put a clean

bandage on it but I think you should get the doctor to check it out, just in case.'

He didn't want to hear the concern lacing her voice.

Her eyes creased in concentration as she carefully placed the bandage over the wound but there was now something less assured about her movements, a faint tremor in her fingers, a shallowness to her breathing. He recognised the sound. Its familiarity was akin to pouring petrol on a flame.

His hands clenched into fists but this time it was not anger he was fighting. It was desire, the desire to run his fingers through that short crop, to trace her cheekbones and the softness of her skin.

Grace cleared her throat. When she spoke her voice was husky. 'All done. Let's take a look at your knuckles.'

She lifted her eyes to meet his and for an instant he was thrown back in time to a place where nothing had existed for them but each other. There was the light sprinkling of freckles across her long nose, the same freckles he had been determined to count every last one of, the small beauty spot on her left cheekbone and the tiny childhood scar above her top lip that was the result of an accident with barbed wire. A thousand memories filled him and the desire to press his lips to hers and capture a taste of that remembered honey sweetness came on the verge of consuming him.

Only the ring of his phone saved him.

Those memories were from a different life when he had been a different man and Grace had been a different woman.

Now she was poison.

Shoving his chair back, he got to his feet and dug his stinging hand into his pocket. *'Ciao.'*

He sighed as he listened to his PA explain about a production problem in the bottling factory.

'I need to go,' he said once he had ended the call. 'We will finish this conversation another time.'

Grace opened her mouth then closed it. Then opened it again. He braced himself for the anticipated insult she was certain to throw at him. The only thing she threw at him was another antiseptic wipe.

'For your knuckles,' she explained tightly. 'And make sure you see your doctor about the wound.'

For the briefest of moments he caught the desolation in her eyes before she straightened and turned her back on him.

Outside in the fresh air he took a moment to compose himself.

If his phone hadn't rung he would have kissed her. And one kiss would never have been enough. He would have wanted all of her.

Swearing under his breath, he strode back to the monastery.

He would not be a slave to his libido. He would master it until he found a mistress who would serve as an outlet for it.

Yet no matter how hard he tried to envisage this mythical woman, the only image that came to his mind was that of his wife.

CHAPTER SIX

GRACE STEPPED INTO the master bedroom with a real sense of trepidation. It was the first time she had been inside it since the day of her return. There was no denying this room was now very much Luca's territory.

Puffing air through her bottom lip, she walked straight to the door that housed her old dressing room and flung it open.

That sense of walking into the past hit her again. The rows of clothing were exactly as she had left them. All that wonderful colour.

She hadn't bought anything colourful since she left Sicily. Part of that had been because she had known his goons would be searching for a woman who wore vivid colours. The main part had been because the lightness in her heart had darkened and she had subconsciously bought clothes that had reflected that darkness. It had been the same darkness that had killed all her creativity.

Would the light ever return?

Had Luca been through her dressing room in her absence, looking for clues as to where she had gone? When he'd finally realised that she'd left him, had he been tempted to throw all her clothes onto a bonfire?

His mother had said he'd kept all her possessions in case she returned to collect them.

No matter how hard she tried to push the image out of her head, all she could see when she closed her eyes was the agony etched across his features when he described the effect her disappearance had had on him.

The raw emotion that had resonated from him had almost sliced her in two.

Surely he didn't really need it spelled out why she had left? Who in their right mind would knowingly bring a child into such a dangerous world? It was different for him. Luca had been born and raised in it. To him, it was normal.

That had been made abundantly clear two days before she'd left.

She'd been in her cottage painting. For the first time ever, the smell of the turpentine she used to clean her brushes and thin her paints had made her queasy. Truth be told, she'd been feeling nauseous for a few days, had assumed she'd picked up a bug. Her usual boundless energy had deserted her too, so she'd decided to call it a day and get an early night.

She hadn't even opened the door to their wing when she heard the shouting.

Luca and Pepe often rowed but this had been a real humdinger of an argument, vicious, their raised voices echoing off the walls of the corridor surrounding Luca's office. A loud smash had made her jump back a foot.

For an age she had stared at the office door wondering whether she should go in and defuse whatever was going on between them or leave them to get on with it. There was always the risk she could walk in to them throwing stuff at each other and inadvertently get caught in the firing line.

Before she could make up her mind, the door had flown open and Pepe had stormed out, almost careering into her.

He'd stopped short. 'Sorry. I didn't know you were there.'

'Don't worry about it,' she'd said. 'Is everything okay?'

A stupid question. Even if she hadn't heard them argue, one look at the thunder on her brother-in-law's face would have answered it.

'Ask your husband,' he had replied curtly.

When he had left their wing, he had slammed the door hard enough for her to feel sorry for its hinges.

She'd entered Luca's office and found him pacing in front of the window, a glass of Scotch in his hand. A large trail of coffee stained one of the white walls, a smashed cup on the carpet below it.

'What's the matter?' she'd asked. 'Who's been throwing inanimate objects at the wall?'

He'd spun around to face her, his features contorted in the same thunderous expression as Pepe's.

'I thought you were in your studio,' he'd snapped.

Unused to having that tone of voice directed at her, she'd flinched.

'I'm sorry,' he'd muttered, shaking his head. 'It's been one of those days.'

'I heard you arguing with Pepe. What was that about?'

'Nothing important.'

'It must have been important that way you two were shouting at each other. And smashing things.' Deliberately, she had kept her tone even, hoping it would be enough to defuse his rage and calm him down enough to talk to her.

'I *said* it was nothing important.' He had downed his Scotch then pulled his jacket from the back of his chair and shrugged his arms into it.

'Where are you going?'

'Out.'

'Out where?'

'I have business to attend to.'

'It's nearly ten o'clock.'

'My business does not conform to office hours.'

'So I've noticed.'

His gaze had snapped to her. 'And what's that supposed to mean?'

'Your long hours used to be here, on the estate, with me. Since you went into partnership with Francesco, I hardly see you, not properly.'

'I'm part owner of two casinos and a handful of night-clubs,' he'd said, speaking through gritted teeth. 'They are nocturnal businesses and need hands-on management.'

'I am well aware of that.'

'Then what are you complaining about?'

'I'm not complaining.' Then her voice had shaken. There had been something so…feral about him at that moment, a wildness that wasn't just due to his unshaven, dishevelled appearance. Luca was usually so perfectly groomed. 'I'm worried about you. You're working too hard. It's not good for you…'

'I shall be the judge of what's good for me,' he had interrupted with a snap. 'You work long hours yourself.'

'And when I'm tired I stop, as I have this evening. You're working yourself into the ground and you're drinking too much. You've been stressed for weeks. Months. Look how you were with me at the casino last night…'

'I've apologised for that.'

'I know, but I still don't know what was going on…'

'Nothing was going on and I would thank you to stop harping on about it!' His voice had risen to a shout. Before she'd had time to blink, he'd swept all the contents of his desk onto the floor where they landed with a clatter.

She had stared at him with wide eyes. Her heart had hammered beneath her ribs. 'What is *wrong* with you?'

'How many times do I have to tell you to stop interfering?' he'd shouted. 'My business dealings are none of your affair.'

'Of course they are—we're married.' She'd always known Luca had a temper on him but it had never been directed at her before; not like this. But she would not back down. Not this time. 'I'm your wife, not a child. You used to talk to me about everything but now you won't confide in me at all, not about anything, not the business, not your argument with your brother, not *anything*.'

He'd thrown his arms in the air. 'I don't have time for this, *bella*. I need to go.'

'Why?' She had backed against the door to block his exit.

'I've already told you. I have work to do.'

She had folded her arms across her chest and said the words she'd longed to say for months. 'No. I want you to stay at home tonight and talk to me. I want you to tell me what the hell's going on in your life that is turning you into a stranger.'

His face a mask of fury, he had stood before her. 'I am not answerable to you, or Pepe, or anyone. I am your husband and my word alone should be good enough to satisfy any curiosity you may have. Now move aside.'

'Or what? You'll manhandle me out of the way?'

He'd raised his eyes to the ceiling and muttered an oath that even Grace with her limited Italian had understood.

Anyone in their right mind would have got out of his way immediately, but no matter how hard her heart had hammered, no matter how frightened she had been, she hadn't been frightened of *him*. No, something else had scared her and however hard she had tried to swat it away, it had loomed closer than ever.

When he'd looked back down at her, his features had regained some form of composure. 'Please, Grace,' he'd said, his voice surprisingly tender. 'You are reading too much into this. All brothers argue. The casinos and night-clubs need hands-on running, that is all.' He had stroked a finger down her cheek. 'How about I promise to stay out no more than a couple of hours? When I get home we'll share a bottle of wine and I'll give you a massage. How does that sound?'

Despite herself, despite knowing she shouldn't just capitulate, she'd nodded and sighed, pressing her forehead against his chest. Luca's heart had been hammering as wildly as her own.

'I worry I don't know you any more,' she'd confessed. 'You're hardly ever home and when you are, you're distant with me. And you're drinking too much—it scares me.'

Wrapping his strong arms tightly around her, he'd buried his face in her hair. 'You have nothing to worry about, *amore*. I swear. You know I love you. That will never change.'

Tears had pricked her eyes, fear gripping her stronger than ever. 'I love you too.'

When he had returned that night, there had been no shared bottle of wine and no massage. Even though her head had ached and her heart had been heavy, she had fallen asleep on the sofa. He'd carried her to their bedroom and helped her undress, then let her sleep, locked in his arms.

In the morning, she had awoken and immediately sat upright, as if she'd been hit by a lightning bolt. He'd already left for work, leaving a sweet note on his pillow for her. He hadn't been there for her to tell of the vivid dream that had awoken her so abruptly. The dream had brought into sharp focus something that had been hovering in the back of her mind for days, like a wispy cloud that refused to be caught.

She'd dreamt she was pregnant.

* * *

'Is there a problem?'

Grace jumped. She'd been so lost in the past, the carpet so thick, she hadn't heard Luca's approach.

She pressed a hand to her chest and managed the faintest of smiles. 'Lily's napping, so I thought I should see if I had anything suitable to wear for the party on Saturday.'

'I'll get a member of staff to move everything to the blue room,' he said, looking past her. 'But I doubt there is anything suitable to wear in there.'

'What do you mean?'

'In the past I was happy to indulge your preference for bright colours but not any more. The party we're attending is a high-society affair and you will dress appropriately.'

'You always liked that I dressed differently. Unless you were lying to me.'

'That was then,' he said coldly. 'I was far too indulgent. I have already stated my desire for a traditional Sicilian wife. In future you shall wear clothes *I* deem appropriate in public.'

'And what does a Sicilian husband deem appropriate wifely apparel for a party with the cream of Florentine society?'

'Something demure, elegant and sedate. And not just in her dress but in her manners too.' He stared at her pointedly.

'You really are full of it,' she said scornfully. 'I would *kill* to see a man try and tell your mother what to wear and how to behave.'

'My father would never have told her how to behave because he loved her for who she was. The simple difference is, I do not love you. Your wants and needs mean nothing to me. When you accompany me as my wife you will wear what I tell you and behave as I tell you or you can pack your bags and leave.'

He meant every word. She could feel it.

If she called his bluff and packed, he would arrange a driver to take her to the edge of the estate. Once at the border, that would be it. She would never be allowed back in.

'In that case, I shall go shopping for the drabbest dress in the world.' She plastered the biggest, fakest smile she could muster to her face. 'I'll do my best to buy a dress that is the epitome of elegance.'

'Rather than rely on your definition of elegance, I will accompany you.' He checked his watch. 'I'll clear my schedule for the next few hours. We can leave now.'

The dress on the mannequin had thin straps and a tight buttercup-yellow bodice that narrowed in a V at the waist. Its skirt fell to the knees at the front, the back flaring down to the ankles like a peacock tail, a riot of reds, yellows and oranges. It was so beautifully designed and cut, so fantastically offbeat that Grace couldn't help but stare wistfully at it.

Luca appeared by her side with a fawning shop assistant. 'I have selected the dresses I wish you to try,' he said in the offhand manner he had adopted since they'd arrived at the exclusive shopping arcade.

Leaving Lily with him, she followed another assistant into the plush changing room.

He'd selected four dresses. Like the others she had already paraded herself in, they were all in varying shades of beige. If there was one colour she loathed, it was beige. She remembered on one of their previous, happier shopping trips she had regaled him for a good twenty minutes about why beige was so nondescript it didn't deserve to be called a colour. Even in her darkest days she would never have contemplated wearing it.

In their marriage's first incarnation, he had made her

feel like a princess whenever they went shopping together, never caring if her preferences were a little offbeat, his only wish for her to feel confident and happy in whatever she chose. This time he dismissed each of her humiliating parades in front of him with a dismissive sweep of his eyes, his attention taken with the fawning shop assistant, who at one point he permitted to hold Lily.

The spike of jealousy that pierced into her chest was so acute she had to fight the urge to rip her child from the assistant's arms.

'Lily will need a bottle soon,' she finally snapped when displaying the fourth dress for him. 'Will this one do?'

He fixed cold eyes on her. 'I think it is highly suitable.'

'Great.' She bestowed him with a saccharine smile and sashayed back into the changing room. Of all the dresses she had tried on, this one was the greatest antithesis to style. It resembled something her grandmother would wear to a wedding.

She had no choice but to suck it up. She would rather die than be parted from her daughter.

Once the dress was packaged and Luca had paid, he led them to a bustling café for a late lunch.

'Can't we go straight home?' Grace asked, in no mood to spend any more time with him. In three days they would be going on an overnight trip to Florence for the blasted party. She was going to be stuck with him for at least twenty-four hours.

'You're the one who said Lily needed another feed.'

Naturally, Lily chose that moment to start grizzling.

Without exchanging another word between them, they ordered. While they waited for their meals, a waiter was dispatched to heat Lily's bottle.

'Why do you not breastfeed?' Luca asked, finally breaking the silence between them.

Rocking Lily on her shoulder, she stared at him. 'Why?'

'It surprises me. I assumed you would want to.'

His accurate assumption turned her stomach. In the early days of their marriage they had agreed that having a baby would be something to embark on in the future. Grace had only been twenty-three. There had been plenty of time. Selfishly, they had wanted to enjoy each other first. Even so, she had become rather slapdash about taking her contraceptive pill.

'Life happens.'

His eyes hardened. 'Considering I have already missed so much of her life, it is only fair that you fill in the blanks.'

She met his gaze. 'You think?'

He leaned forward. 'I want to know everything about our child. Everything. In due course you will tell me, but for now you can start with why you did not breastfeed.'

Grace was interrupted from glaring at him when the waiter returned with Lily's bottle.

'Well?' Luca said, impatient, once the waiter had left them.

'I couldn't breastfeed,' she said flatly, shifting Lily's position and putting the teat in her mouth. 'The midwives wanted to help but they were too busy. Nothing we tried worked. I was exhausted, Lily was hungry…' She shrugged. 'In the end they had to discharge me because they needed the bed, so Lily and I went home and onto formula milk.'

'Just think,' he said, his voice musing but his eyes like a frozen winter night. 'If you'd had your husband there to take the burden off you, the outcome might have been different.'

'You'd love to think that, wouldn't you?' She shook her head with a grimace. 'The big hero riding to the rescue of his wife's underperforming breasts. Tell me,' she continued, ignoring the throbbing pulse in his temple, which always meant danger, 'how exactly would you have helped? Unless biology has advanced to allow you to lactate, I don't see what possible help you could have given me.'

'I would have been there for both of you. I would have taken care of Lily so you could sleep and recover. Who was there for you, Grace? When you gave birth to our child, who was there for you? Who was there to help you recover?'

Cheeks burning, she gazed down at her guzzling baby.

He leaned forward again. 'You can justify it all you want but you made the first three months of Lily's life an unnecessary struggle for you both.'

She turned her head and stared pointedly at their bodyguards who were sitting at the table next to them. 'Our freedom from you and from them made the struggles necessary. And for all your talk about "being there" for us, don't think it's escaped my attention that you haven't held her yet. Not once. While I've spent the morning acting as a prancing clothes horse, you've spent your time flirting with the shop assistants.'

'You sound jealous.'

'Don't change the subject.'

'There is nothing more unattractive than a jealous wife.'

'And there's nothing more unattractive than a married man flirting with another woman in front of his wife and baby.'

'I was not flirting—'

'And you can't expect me to believe Sicilian women don't get jealous,' she continued, deliberately talking over him. 'How would your mother have reacted if your father had flirted with younger women?'

'She would have pulled his testicles off with her fingernails.' He smiled coldly. 'But my father adored her, so he never needed or wanted a mistress.'

The waiter arrived with their steaming plates of pasta, suppressing her urge to punch Luca in the face.

She wanted to hurt him. Right then she wanted to make him suffer for everything he had put her through, was putting her through, and everything she would have to endure for the next eighteen years. Unless she found an escape route. Which she would.

While she finished feeding Lily, Luca ate his pasta and caught up on his emails, effectively blanking her out.

'Have you even spoken to Lily yet?'

He raised his eyes.

'Have you?' She carefully placed the baby on her shoulder and patted her bottom.

'Babies can't talk.'

'Have you tried *any* form of interaction with her?'

His nostrils flared. 'Lily does not yet know me. I have no wish to upset her.'

'You were happy to let the shop assistant—a stranger—hold her.'

He shrugged. 'She asked.'

'On that basis, you would let any random person who wanted to hold our child have her?'

'Only the ones I find attractive enough to consider making my mistress.'

She flinched. 'So you *were* flirting.'

'I wouldn't call it *flirting*. I would call it *auditioning*.'

'You're really enjoying this, aren't you?'

'I take no pleasure from humiliating people. In your case I am prepared to make an exception.' He took a bite of pasta and cast his eyes back down to his tablet.

'That's funny.'

'What is?'

'You saying you get no pleasure from humiliating people. In your line of work I would have thought humiliation was a perk.'

That got his attention. He put his fork down. His narrowed eyes captured hers. 'My line of work?'

'You're a gangster. A criminal.'

CHAPTER SEVEN

GRACE COULD HAVE sworn Luca blanched, but, it was such a fleeting expression, one blink and it had gone.

'I am not a criminal.'

'Really?' She made no attempt to hide her disbelief. 'How would you describe yourself?'

'I'm a businessman.'

'Hmm. So it's normal behaviour for businessmen to live in the Sicilian equivalent of Fort Knox and travel everywhere with armed guards? Is it also normal for businessmen to beat people?'

His eyes had blackened, his nostrils flared. 'What, exactly, do you mean by that?'

'Do you remember a couple of days or so before I left you, I went with you to the casino? Do you remember when I walked into the office and that man was in there with you all? Do you remember him? Because I do. Even though you marched me out straight away, I got a good look at his face. I saw that man a few days later in Palermo. Both of his arms had been broken and his face looked as if he'd been in a boxing match against an opponent twice his size.'

While she had no time for Luca's nightclubs, she'd liked spending time in his casinos, especially the one in Palermo. She'd come to enjoy their nights out there, dining in the à la carte restaurant and playing cards. The night she had been referring to had been their last night out together. She had been playing poker, a game she was good at, but her frequent yawns had got the better of her. She'd wanted to go home and go to bed, preferably with her husband.

Luca had been nowhere to be found on the gaming floor, so she had wandered off to the security offices on the top floor. Being one of the bosses' wives meant she had access to anywhere she desired.

She had found him in the nondescript office used by the duty manager.

The man in question had been sitting in a chair in the middle of the room surrounded by Luca, Francesco and two men she didn't know. Those two men, with their broken noses and cauliflower ears, had given her the heebie-jeebies.

She could still taste the testosterone of that office, could still feel the menacing atmosphere that had greeted her when she walked through the door.

All the men had fixed their eyes on her, their surprise that she'd barged in on them palpable.

'Everything all right?' she had asked with a naivety she looked back on with disgust.

'We're in the middle of a meeting,' Luca had said curtly, striding over to her.

'Are you going to be much longer? Only I'm tired and want to go home.'

'We will not be long.' He'd taken her arm and ushered her to the door. 'Wait for me in the bar. I'll be with you shortly.'

He'd shut her out before she could make a whisper of protest.

She'd stared at the offending door for too long, an uneasiness creeping through her bones to go with the shock of her own husband frogmarching her from the room. There had been something about the man in the chair's expression that kept flashing through her mind.

When she had challenged Luca about it on the drive home, he'd dismissed the matter, refusing to discuss it.

She'd dropped the subject but the man in the chair had haunted her. The more she'd thought about it, the more convinced she'd become that it had been a pleading terror she had seen in his eyes.

A couple of days later she had walked out of a pharmacy in Lebbrossi and come face to face with him. He'd almost fallen into the road in his haste to get away from her.

She'd watched him hurry away, utterly bewildered. Stuffed in the bottom of her handbag, away from the prying eyes of her minders, had been a pregnancy test.

'That man was cheating the casino,' Luca said, finally breaking the silence that had sprung between them.

'And?' She was being deliberately facetious. She wanted him to spell it out to her. She wanted to watch him justify breaking the bones of a fellow human being.

'And here in Sicily we have our own methods for dealing with people who try to cheat us,' he said coolly. 'Lessons need to be learned.'

'That was one hell of a lesson. That poor man recognised me as your wife. I swear he looked as if he'd come face to face with the Medusa.'

'That *poor man* stole over a hundred thousand euros from us.'

'Ooh, yes, I can totally see how that would justify smashing his face in.' Sick to the pit of her stomach, Grace shook her head. Her tortellini had gone cold but she didn't care. Her appetite had deserted her.

'Believe me, he got off lightly.'

'Lightly? *Lightly?* What planet are you on? How can you even try to justify—?'

'Rules are rules, and breaking them merits punishment, as that man knew very well. He didn't just steal from us, he dishonoured us. He's lucky I'm a reasonable man and refused to counter a harsher punishment.'

She stared at him open-mouthed. *A harsher punishment...?*

'That man had a family,' he continued. 'At my insistence we agreed to give him time to repay the money. But we couldn't let him leave without serving a warning, not just to him but to any other man foolish enough to try and steal from us.'

She shook her head again, trying to make sense of it all. 'So what you're saying is, you took me home and made love to me that night, minutes after beating him.'

'No. I never raised a finger to him.' The corners of his mouth lifted slightly. 'I had a wife I wished to take home and make love to.'

'You might not have *raised a finger* to him but your hands are still tainted with his blood.'

The half-smile dropped. 'This isn't a school playground, Grace.'

'Isn't it? From what I remember of school, it was always the bullies who ruled the roost. And you wonder why I ran away from you when I found out I was pregnant? Who in their right mind would bring a child into this life?'

His eyes blackened. It was like looking into an abyss.

Lily had dozed off on her shoulder, for which she would be eternally grateful. This was not a conversation she wanted her daughter to hear even if she was far too young to understand it.

Surprisingly, being in a public place made the whole thing easier. It meant she had to keep a rein on herself. It meant Luca had to keep his control too.

Taking a deep breath, she forced her attention back on

him. At moments like this it pained her heart to look at him, physically hurt to recall how deeply she had loved him.

It hurt even more to know that, despite everything he had done, he still had the power to affect her more than anyone. Deep inside her existed an ache to turn back the clock, to have stayed at home that fateful day, to stick her head back in the sand. To be happy again.

But Pandora's box, once opened, could not be unopened. She had seen that poor man's face and she had *known*.

Luca's secretiveness. The increased security detail that had already been large enough to shame a head of state. His growing reluctance to let her even leave the estate, never mind go anywhere without him. These were all things that had festered but were forgotten about the minute she was with him. When they were together, making love, and she knew she was the centre of his earth, she would forget all her doubts.

She would forget her worries about his drinking and how a glass of Scotch seemed to be permanently welded to his hand. She'd pretend not to see days of unshaven thick black stubble across his strong jawline. She'd pretend not to notice the wildness that resided in his eyes when she caught him in an unguarded moment.

Ironically enough, since he'd found her again, lookswise it was like being back with the Luca she had married rather than the Luca she had left. But that wildness in his eyes remained. That edge to him that had been there from the start—the same edge she had thought *romantic*—was as strong as it had ever been. Stronger. His hate for her sharpening it to a point.

The pink line of the pregnancy test had shone brightly. In that split second it had no longer been just her and Luca. A tiny spark of life had resided within her, depending on *her*.

Denial had no longer been an option.

She'd forced herself to work on autopilot. She'd left without writing a note because trying to say goodbye to the man she loved had ripped her soul into pieces.

She'd run so fast, she'd never had the chance to ask him any of the million and one questions that had pounded in her head. Those questions still pounded.

'Have you ever used *your* fists on another man?'

'Only when it's been absolutely necessary.'

'But what do you consider necessary?'

His voice was hard. 'People who steal and cheat from me. People who would harm my family. People who would try to take my businesses from me.'

'Have you ever killed someone?' The question was out before her brain had even conjured it.

For the briefest of moments, his jaw slackened, before all his muscles bunched. 'How can you ask me such a question?'

'Because I don't know you.' She hugged Lily closer to her. Never had she wished so hard that she'd moved on from Cornwall when she'd had the chance. If that ridiculous apathy hadn't overcome her she'd likely be living on a remote Greek island away from this madness. 'You *changed*, Luca. Once you went into business with that Francesco Calvetti, you changed. The darkness seemed to take you over. I was walking on eggshells all the time, always wondering and worrying over what kind of a mood you were in. I would spend nights in my studio painting and trying to ignore how terrified I was that you wouldn't come home…'

'Why would you have thought that?'

'Because people in your line of work have a habit of not making it home. Except for in a coffin.'

'My line of work?' Anger rose in his voice. 'I am a legitimate businessman.'

'You're nothing but a thug,' she countered flatly. 'Only I was too blind with love or lust to see it properly.'

A snarl flittered across his face, the pulse in his temple pounding. Pulling his wallet out of his back pocket, Luca rose and threw some euros onto the table. 'Put Lily in her pram. We're leaving.'

Luca had been in bed for the best part of two hours. For two nights, sleep had been a joke. It was worse than when he had first brought Grace home. Try as he might, he could not get her out of his head. Or excise the poison that had spilled from her tongue.

In sheer frustration he threw the sheets off and climbed out of bed. Drawing back the curtain, he stared out of the window at the moonlit view of his estate.

At that moment all was peaceful, the dark rolling hills giving the illusion the vines and olive groves were in deep sleep. He could almost believe he was the only person awake in the whole of Sicily.

Except Grace could be awake too. He'd heard her a while ago, tending to their daughter. She might very well be staring out of her own window, sharing the same view.

His chest tightened and he swallowed away the acid burn in the back of his throat.

She was probably plotting her next attempt to escape with Lily.

She would never succeed. But still she would try.

Her bravery had stood out the first moment he met her. She had trespassed on his land with her best friend. As soon as they had crossed the boundary, an alert had gone out. A camera had zoomed in on the area and they had been spotted. It had been sheer fortune—or misfortune, depending on your take—that Luca had been driving through the estate with his head of security, Paolo, and had been first on the scene. The intruders had been sitting on a picnic blanket, looking as if they didn't have a care in the world.

'Che ci fate qui?' he had said, asking what they were doing while removing his gun from its holster. He had not sensed any danger from these young women but he would not take chances. While Salvatore Calvetti lived and breathed, the Mastrangelos would never be safe.

One of them, a curvy redhead, had jumped up in terror at the sight of the gun but the other, a slender blonde, had stayed on her bottom and gazed up at him. After a moment's study, she had raised one hand in the sign of peace and then dived into her rucksack from which she had retrieved a battered notebook.

'Uno minuti per favore,' she had muttered as she got to her feet, flicking through her book. 'Er...*mi dispiace, ma il mio italiano non è molto buono.*' When she'd finished her garbled apology for not speaking Italian she'd beamed at him.

He'd taken in her tall, lithe frame, her long honey-blonde hair, the bare, dirty feet and the garish multicoloured top over the pair of frayed denim shorts. For all her grubbiness she'd shone brighter than the blazing midday sun.

'Are you English?' he'd asked, putting the gun back in its holster.

She had nodded.

'This is private land. You must leave.'

'I'm sorry,' she had said. 'We didn't realise we were trespassing. There's a gap in your fence we thought was a footpath.'

He had followed the direction she'd pointed at, and had seen a couple of panels had come off.

'Get that fixed,' he'd said to Paolo, who was hovering in the background, before turning his attention back to the striking woman before him. 'You must leave now.'

'Give us a minute to pack our materials away.' She had turned to her cowering friend who was hiding behind her. 'Are you going to stand there like a stuck lemon or are you going to pull your finger out?'

'He's got a gun!' the friend had yelped, pointing a finger at Luca.

'He's also put it away,' she had replied patiently, throwing Luca a discreet wink. That wink had jolted him to his core. 'We are trespassing in Sicily, Cara, not Surrey.'

It was only when they had started packing their stuff away that he'd realised what they had been doing. 'You are artists?'

'I suppose we are,' had said the brave woman, who had not so much as flinched at the sight of his gun. 'We graduated last summer and have been travelling Europe ever since. We're trying to get in as much art appreciation as we can before the real world drags us into its tentacles. That's why we were pitched up here—Cara dabbles in landscapes and the view was spectacular. Honestly, your estate is *beautiful*.'

But Luca had had no interest in Cara. 'Do you paint too?'

'I do. Portraits. I normally work with oil but as we're outdoors I've brought my sketchbook with me.'

'May I see it?'

'Sure.' She had knelt down for another rummage in her rucksack, giving him a perfect view of her pert bottom.

He had blinked in shock as a stab of lust had run through him.

Grubby urchins were usually well off his radar.

This woman though…

She had brought a large sketchbook over to him.

Taking his time, he had flipped through it. Most of the drawings had been of her companion. They had been, without exception, exquisite.

He had looked back up and met her eyes properly for the first time.

The most enormous feeling of warmth had spread through his bones, a thickening in his chest that had made it hard to catch a breath.

'Do you take commissions?' he had asked after too long a pause during which they had simply stared at each other.

Her wide hazel eyes had crinkled at the sides. 'Not from people whose names I don't know.'

He had extended a hand. 'I'm Luca Mastrangelo.'

'Grace Holden.' She had wiped her hand down the side of her shorts before reaching out to accept his.

A shock of heat had zipped through his hand, permeating through him. 'It is a pleasure to meet you, Grace Holden.'

Her answering smile had stolen his remaining breath.

Neither had made any attempt to relinquish the other's hand.

Later, over a romantic meal at his favourite restaurant, he'd asked why she hadn't been scared when he had pulled out the gun.

She'd smiled mischievously. 'You weren't aiming it at us. You looked peed off but not murderous.'

Out of everything, that was the thing that cut in his craw the most. How could the woman who had judged him so accurately with one glance even dream he was capable of murder? Why the hell did she think they had let that man live? It had been at *his* insistence, that was why. That man had been caught cheating from them before, from their casino in Sardinia. Francesco's men had been ready to tow him out to sea and throw him in with weights on his ankles.

Did she think he *enjoyed* hurting people or having people hurt in his name?

He took no more enjoyment from it than his father had.

A lump formed in his throat. Pietro Mastrangelo had been a fine and honourable man who believed in the sanctity of life. Always he would favour the route that left the least physical and emotional damage, a lesson Luca had taken to heart.

The way Grace had looked at him, the words she had said to him…she truly believed him to be a monster. She gave him no credit for saving that man's life. Thanks to him, that man would still be able to live a long life and be a husband to his wife and a father to his children.

She had been happy to leave him, Luca, unable to be a husband *or* a father.

A wave of bitterness ran through him as he recalled her attempts to deflect her deplorable behaviour by turning it onto him.

He made no apologies for restricting her movements and keeping her in the dark on certain matters. He had been doing his best to keep her safe. He would do anything—*would have done anything*, he corrected himself—to keep her safe. He hadn't wanted her to worry about things she could never understand. That was what he'd told himself.

The sound of Lily's cries carried down the corridor and into his room.

Grace's accusation came back to him. *Have you tried* any *form of interaction with her?*

Before he met Grace, he'd never imagined he would marry a woman and selfishly want to keep her all for himself, even if just for a while. With Grace, he'd wanted to enjoy every minute they had together before they got around to making lots of bouncing *bambini*. When those mythical babies eventually came along he'd known he would want to be involved in everything. Their children would be born of their parents' love and would want for nothing, from either their mother or their father.

Grace had stolen that from him.

If she had her way she would steal it from him again.

He rubbed his eyes, the sound of Lily's cries ripping into his heart.

'Don't think it's escaped my attention that you haven't held her yet. Not once.'

She was right.

The way he was acting around his own flesh and blood, anyone would think he was scared of her.

How could a baby be construed as even vaguely frightening? Especially when that baby was *his* child.

He left his room and moved stealthily down the dark corridor to the nursery.

Grace's eyes widened when he walked through the door. 'What's the matter?' she whispered, pacing the room, rocking Lily on her shoulder.

The breath caught in his throat.

His wife and daughter. Together. Illuminated by the moonlight seeping through a crack in the heavy curtains, Grace wearing her tatty dressing gown, Lily bundled up in blankets, her whimpers lessening.

It was a sight he knew he would never tire of gazing at.

He cleared his throat, taking in the dark rings circling his wife's eyes. 'When did you last have a proper night's sleep?'

Her brow furrowed, a flash of pain contorting her features. 'About eleven months ago.'

When she had left him.

And just like that, he understood what terrible anguish she must have gone through.

Whatever her reasoning had been, and whatever vitriol she might spout now, it hadn't been any easier for Grace to break their union than it had been for him to accept that she had left of her own accord.

She hadn't left because she no longer loved him.

She had left *despite* it.

Dio, but he had no idea how that made him feel.

'Can I hold her?' He hadn't meant to ask. He'd intended to simply take Lily from her. After all, he was the father. It was his right.

She didn't say anything, her tired eyes simply gazing at him with more than a hint of apprehension. Eventually she inclined her head.

'Aren't you going to give me any tips about keeping her head supported, or anything?' he could not resist asking as he stood before her.

A faint trace of a smile curved her lips, a smile that did something all squidgy to his chest, before it faded away and he detected sadness in its place. 'You'd never hurt her.'

She delivered it as a whimsical statement of fact. The squidgy feeling became a tight mass.

Between them they transferred Lily into his arms, the tight mass solidifying into a heavy weight, spreading up his throat and down into his guts, enveloping his insides. The softness of Grace pressed against his arm, her clean fragrance filling his senses, all of this merged with the plump delicacy of his daughter and the new baby scent that was all her own.

For a moment he couldn't breathe, the feelings evoked so powerful they threatened to overwhelm him.

Lily stopped grizzling. She stared up at him, her midnight eyes almost curious, as if she were trying to work out who this stranger was who now held her so protectively.

Grace watched them, the ray of moonlight casting her in an ethereal light, emphasising both her beauty and her tiredness.

'You need to sleep,' he said, lowering himself onto the rocking chair next to Lily's cot. 'Go to bed. I'll get her back down.'

She opened her mouth, no doubt to argue with him, but all that came out was an enormous yawn, which she covered with the back of her hand.

'If I have any problems I'll wake you.'

Still she hesitated before giving a short nod. 'Okay. If you're sure?'

'I'm sure.'

She closed the space between them and leaned over, placing her lips to their daughter's cheek, her hair inadvertently tickling his throat. 'Sleep tight, my angel.'

As she made to straighten up she wobbled slightly and placed a hand on his bare thigh to steady herself.

'Sorry,' she murmured, taking a step back.

'Don't be.' His skin heated, and he breathed deeply, willing the completely inappropriate feelings to disperse.

She backed up to the adjoining door. 'Well, goodnight, then.'

'Goodnight, *bella*.'

Alone with his daughter, Luca closed his eyes and breathed in Lily's sweet scent. The heavy weight inside him had become a pulsating ball of steel and it took long moments before he felt ready to properly look at her.

Carefully he laid her on his lap and stared, taking in the long limbs, the skinny fingers, the plump cheeks, the snub nose, everything. The longer he looked, the harder it became to breathe.

His daughter. His flesh and blood.

CHAPTER EIGHT

WHEN GRACE AWOKE, she checked the time on her bedside clock and almost fell out of bed in shock.

Throwing the covers off, she jumped out and raced into the adjoining nursery, completely skipping the blurry-eyed, lots-of-yawning routine the morning usually brought.

The cot was empty.

Pressing a hand to her racing heart, she gnawed at her bottom lip and forced her frantic brain to calm down and think.

She checked in the small fridge she'd had placed in the corner of the room. Instead of the two made-up bottles of Lily's milk she'd put in there before going to bed, there was only one.

Still chewing on her lip, she headed off along the corridor. Was it possible Luca had heard Lily call for her breakfast while she had slept through it? Surely not? Her bedroom adjoined the nursery, and her maternal biology was primed to hear her baby's cries.

The door to the master bedroom was ajar. She tapped on it lightly. Getting no response, she tapped again then pushed it open.

Rooted to the floor, all she could do was stare, wide-eyed.

Luca was asleep on the edge of the ultra-king bed. Lily

lay on her back next to him, bang in the middle, wearing a sleep suit Grace was certain she hadn't been wearing when she'd put her to bed. A pile of pillows had been placed neatly along the other edge, sandwiching Lily between them and Luca. On his bedside table sat an empty baby bottle.

Heart in mouth, she swallowed away the compulsion to climb in with them, stood for an age unable to tear her eyes away.

Her presence must have disturbed him, for Luca raised his head. 'What time is it?'

She cleared her throat. 'Nine o'clock.'

As he sat up she noticed how careful he was not to use any sudden movements that could wake Lily. All the same, the baby stirred and kicked her little feet out.

Now fully upright, his black hair mussed, Luca reached for Lily and cuddled her to his bare chest. From Grace's vantage point she could see the wound on his shoulder—the wound *she* had inflicted—was healing well, now a dark red scar. It made her stomach roll to know every time he looked in a mirror and saw that scar, he would be reminded of the time she had shot him.

At the same time fresh guilt was kicking in, her mouth ran dry as she experienced a pang of envy, not that Lily had evidently accepted him without question, but envy that he held her so tenderly.

How Grace had loved to nestle into that broad chest…

'What time did she wake up for her bottle?' she asked, pushing all thoughts of nibbling at his nipples and running her fingers through his black silky hair from her mind.

'A couple of hours ago.' He yawned widely.

'I never heard her.'

'She fell asleep not long after you went back to bed, but as soon as I put her down she woke up and started crying. I didn't want her to wake you, so I decided the best thing to ensure you got a decent amount of sleep was to bring her to bed with me.' He shrugged nonchalantly. 'The bed is big enough.'

That it certainly was.

'Er, well, thank you.'

'I do not require your gratitude,' he said, a touch frostily. 'I *want* to be involved in her care. Besides, it gave you a chance to catch up on some needed sleep.'

She stared at him, too shocked that he'd done something for her partial benefit to speak.

'Which is why our trip to Florence tomorrow could not come at a more opportune moment,' he continued. 'It will do you good to have some space. I'm guessing you've not spent much time apart from her since she was born?'

'Of course I haven't.' Other than her one visit to her cottage studio, she had never been parted from their daughter. She could only tolerate Lily being in the next room by leaving the adjoining door wide open. Which was why it shocked her that she had been able to sleep so deeply. Was it because she knew Lily was in Luca's care…?

He had cared for her beautifully. That much she had to acknowledge. Though she didn't want to. When she looked at Luca she wanted to know she was looking at a bastard, not at a man with the capacity to tend for a young baby on instinct alone.

And now she needed to take Lily back to the nursery and get her ready for the day. And that meant taking her from him. It meant having to get close to his naked chest—*Please, God, let him at least be wearing a pair of boxer shorts.*

As ridiculous as she knew it to be, she had to practically drag her legs over to his side of the bed. Holding her breath, she leaned down and took Lily from his arms.

'What are your plans for the day?' he asked as she took a step back.

'We'll probably go for a walk.' It was on the tip of her tongue to question why he asked, but she stopped herself in time. The last thing she wanted was for him to invite himself along.

Unsurprisingly, his eyes narrowed with suspicion. The only time in the whole of their marriage she had voluntarily gone for a walk and not been badgered into it had been the day she left him. 'Another walk?'

She shrugged. 'It's not for me, it's for Lily. She needs fresh air and I really can't have a SWAT team accompanying us if we leave the estate. Yesterday was bad enough.' The day before, she had taken Lily into Palermo for some Christmas shopping. She hadn't visited the discreet arcade Luca had taken her to to buy the vile dress, but went to a proper shopping centre and market. It had been so crowded her bodyguards had been tripping over the heels of her feet to keep up with them.

'The minders I have assigned to you are discreet.'

'About as discreet as a herd of cows dressed in pink tutus.'

His lips twitched. 'I'm sorry if you find them an inconvenience,' he said without sounding the slightest bit apologetic, 'but as I have explained to you countless times, they're for your safety.'

'Absolutely.' She nodded with faux sweetness. 'It was much harder to tolerate when I thought you were a legitimate businessman and an overprotective bear. But now I know it's all because you're worried one of your victims will get vengeance by going for me and Lily, it makes your attitude so much easier to sympathise with.'

The humour vanished from his face. He climbed off the bed and stalked towards her, a furrow running down the centre of his brow. He wore nothing but a pair of snug black boxer shorts. All the breath in her lungs expelled in a rush.

Luca, virtually naked, was as stunning a sight as if he had been fully nude. He was the only person for whom she had ever wished she were more proficient in sculpture, his body deserving to be immortalised on something even more substantial than canvas.

'My business activities have nothing to do with my security provisions other than in respect of the scumbags it occasionally forces me to associate with. There are no *victims*.'

She averted her gaze from the wonder that was his body and forced herself to meet his eyes. That was no safer place to look, his eyes holding her like a magnet. No matter how hard she tried to look away, she could not.

This physical weakness for him enraged her and she could feel angry colour stain her cheeks. 'You can tell me this until you're blue in the face, but nothing is going to convince me you are anything but a gangster.'

Luca's rage was like a tight coil. She could see it in the way his muscles bunched under his smooth skin.

Her breath hitched.

'You are lucky you can use Lily as a shield,' he said, his silky voice menacing, 'or I would be forced to silence your vicious tongue.'

'That sounds like a threat.'

'Not at all, *bella*. As you should know, I never make useless threats, only promises. If you keep challenging me I will have no option but to shut you up the only way I know that works with you.'

'Oh, yes? And how's that, Gangster Boy?' Why was she antagonising him so? Why could she not simply keep her mouth shut and walk away?

He studied her for an age, the fury in his eyes dispersing and being replaced by a gleam that frightened her a whole lot more than mere anger. Suddenly she was all too aware of the shortness of her nightdress—in her rush to find Lily she'd forgotten to put on her dressing gown.

His olive throat moved; his magnificent chest rose.

She could hear the heaviness of her own breathing, knew he was close enough to hear it too. He was too close. She could smell the musky scent of his skin…

'By kissing you.'

'Now you're being ridiculous.'

He took another step towards her, stopping just short of touching her. But it was enough. The heat of his naked skin so close to hers was enough to make her traitorous body, already wholly aware with her skin tingling and her blood thick and warm, spring alive.

'Ridiculous?' His voice dropped to a murmur. 'Do you not remember how good it used to be between us?'

She shivered, unwanted yet, oh, so potent images of just how good they had been together flittering in her head. 'I thought you were on the hunt for a mistress.'

'So did I.' His eyes were stark with a desire she recognised from old, his voice barely audible. 'But you are the only woman who can make me hard with a single look. And you want me too—I can see it in your eyes. I *know* you, Grace. And I know when you want me. If Lily wasn't in your arms we would already be on that bed screwing each other's brains out.'

The air thickened with the same tightening as in her core. Struggling for oxygen, she fought to make her vocal cords work. 'Don't say another word. You can keep hunting because there is no way I'm *ever* sharing a bed with you again. I don't want you—I *hate* you.'

She turned on her heel and fled, hurrying all the way back to the hateful blue room, a room she loathed almost as much as she loathed her husband. She let the door shut with a slam.

Holding Lily to her, she sat on the bed and waited for her thundering heart to slow to at least near normal levels, berating herself for her stupidity.

Thank God she'd had Lily in her arms. There had been a moment when her fingers had itched to slap him while her lips had tingled to kiss him.

To do more than kiss him.

Why had she not had the good sense to take Lily back to her room immediately, without striking up a conversation with him, without antagonising him?

Deep down, she knew why.

Seeing Luca and Lily together had disturbed her on so many levels she'd had to fight, lest the softening in her bones became a permanent thing.

They had looked so…so…perfect together. Seeing them like that… The guilt had almost split her in two.

Then, when Luca had woken, his defences against her down, his hatred still sleeping, he had looked exactly like the man she had married.

She didn't want to remember anything good about him. She didn't want to remember how convinced she had once been that he would make a fantastic father, even if his offspring would be unable to breathe without his knowledge.

He had been more of a father to Lily in one night than her own father had been to Grace in her entire lifetime.

It had been hard enough to leave Luca the first time. How easy would it be to leave if Lily fell in love with him too? She had to remember the man he had become by the end of their marriage. The man she had run away from.

She cast her mind to the cheap phone currently stuffed in a pair of boots in her wardrobe.

She didn't know how it could help in her escape plan

but just having something that was hers and untraceable felt precious.

If Luca found it, she would be thrown out on the streets. It made no difference that he still wanted her. That was just chemistry. He didn't love her. He would cast her out as if she were nothing more than uneaten food.

She couldn't quite believe she'd been able to acquire it. She hadn't gone shopping with the intention of buying a phone—her only intention had been to buy her mum and Cara a Christmas present each; something to let them know how special they were to her. To make amends.

Not that Billie thought there was anything to make amends for. When she'd spoken to her mum, it was as if she'd never been away—Billie had made some appropriate-sounding noises of relief and appropriate squeals at being a grandmother before discussing, in great detail, her latest commission. By all accounts Grace's dad was somewhere in Africa with no plans to return any time soon. If he knew or cared that she'd been missing, she didn't know. And she didn't ask. Some questions were better left unasked.

Cara's reaction to Grace's reappearance had been somewhat different. Other than a couple of vague text messages, her best friend was being decidedly elusive. She couldn't blame her, not after she'd been so flippant about Cara's fright the day they'd first met Luca. Cara had been the one with the sense to be frightened of a man with a gun. And somehow Cara had been the one tricked into giving up her phone so the secrets contained within it could be revealed.

Her three bodyguards had been glued to her side for the whole trip until she had come to a bustling market. One stall had sold scarves. Out of the corner of her eye she had noticed a row of cheap phones behind the busy seller's table.

Snatching the opportunity, she had grabbed a scarf, given the pram to her bodyguards and dived into the throng.

When she had reached the front of the table, the crowd thick behind her, she could only hope her guards didn't have X-ray vision. She'd quickly wrapped the phone inside the scarf and, acting as casual as a woman whose heart rate had quadrupled could, placed her purchases in Lily's large baby bag.

She could only pray Luca never found it.

Luca knocked on the door to the blue room. He was confident that, given a little more time, he would start thinking of it as Grace's room. He was also confident that, given a little more time, he would stop thinking of the master bedroom as *their* room.

He ignored the thought that he'd had well over ten months to stop thinking of it as theirs.

When there was still no response, he pushed the door open. Neither Grace nor Lily were anywhere to be found. A small suitcase lay closed on the bed, the dress he had bought her draped over it as if it had been thrown there without any thought. The fancy box it had been perfectly folded into at the boutique had been thrown in the waste bin.

She hated that dress. Really hated it. It had given him a perverse pleasure buying it for her, knowing she would have to obey his wishes and wear it. He had seen it as a fitting punishment for a woman who thrived on colour and light, one of many punishments she would have to endure.

Turning to leave, he caught sight of his reflection in the full-length mirror and stopped short, suddenly certain he had seen a pair of horns sprouting from his head. He blinked to clear the image.

It was just him. Luca.

Not the monster Grace was adamant he had become.

For a moment though…

What did she see when she looked at him?

Did she really see a man with horns on his head?

An image of his tiny, defenceless daughter floated into his head. Lily was an innocent, dependent on the adults who cared for her. She had no voice.

But one day she would. One day she would be old enough to form her own opinions. If she was anything like her mother, those opinions would be contrary to his. Would his daughter look at him and see a monster, an ogre…?

Another, equally powerful thought occurred to him.

What would his father say if he could see him now?

His father. The man who had gone to such great lengths to leave the old life—indeed had taken the final necessary steps mere months before his great heart had failed.

Would his father see a monster too? Would his father understand the route he, Luca, had taken? Would he understand his need to strike out on his own, to step out from under Pietro Mastrangelo's shadow and do something for *him*, to form partnerships and invest in businesses that were nothing to do with family, or vineyards, or olive groves?

When his father had died, all of Luca's dreams of founding his own business empire had died a death with him. He'd had to step into the breach. There had been no other choice, unless you considered letting the estate fall to ruins a choice.

His mother had fallen to pieces. His brother had been about to head off to university. None of the uncles or aunts in his family had been in a position to help, not for any substantial length of time.

That had left him, Luca, to bury his own grief and step into the breach. With one hand he'd learned the ropes while the other hand had been busy keeping at bay the vultures, led by Salvatore Calvetti, who would snatch the estate from them.

For thirteen years he had done nothing but push the estate onwards, investing surplus profits into new vineyards and olive groves across Southern Europe and beyond, new bottling plants, new everything, in the process making the Mastrangelos billionaires.

For thirteen years he'd done his duty.

It was only seeing the world through Grace's enchanted eyes that had propelled him to get out of the rut he hadn't even known he was in.

Francesco Calvetti had been as relieved at the death of his father, a man who would as soon slit your throat as give you the time of day, as Luca had been. Salvatore's death had freed them both, and it had allowed them to rekindle their old friendship. Like Luca, Francesco was ready to take a different path and strike out on his own.

Along with a chain of international restaurants Luca had bought out in his own right, he and Francesco had invested in a couple of casinos and a handful of high-end nightclubs together. That these particular investments required a management technique that differed from his usual management style had not been something Luca had considered before laying his cash on the table.

Once he had understood it, however, he'd gone along with it with little more than a shrug. And if Francesco had embraced these techniques with an enthusiasm that proved more than a little of Salvatore lived on in him, then so be it. This was the way of the world here. It was how his own father had once been forced to conduct business. It was a method Luca understood. He was not averse to using his fists and other weapons to protect himself and his property, had employed numerous tactics throughout the years to keep Salvatore and his henchmen at bay. This situation was no different: you did what was needed to be done to protect your investments and if that meant sending a physical warning to thieves and swindlers, then so be it.

He would never pretend to like it. There were days when, if he was being honest with himself, he would admit that he despised it. He would never pretend it didn't require a strong stomach, but Scotch was a good settler. Especially a couple of large Scotches.

His father might not be happy with his eldest son's choice of investment and even less happy with his choice of business partner, but surely he would understand. Wouldn't he...?

The acidic churning in his guts answered that question for him.

And what would Pietro say if he knew his firstborn son was forcing his own wife to wear a dress she hated out of a perverse sense of punishment and revenge? Would he understand that...?

'What do you want?'

Grace stood in the doorway, Lily in her arms, glaring at him.

'I wanted to remind you that you'll need to be ready to leave after breakfast tomorrow.'

She rolled her eyes and walked past him, placing Lily on the centre of the bed. Immediately their daughter stuffed a foot in her mouth.

'Where have you been?'

'Running through some stuff with your mum about Lily's routine.' She sat on the bed and placed a hand on the baby's belly.

'Any problems?'

'No. She's all good to go.'

Which is more than you are, he thought. Grace looked wan. 'Are you feeling all right?'

'Me?' She smiled tightly. 'I'm absolutely fine. On top of the world. Leaving my daughter for the first time fills me with nothing but joy.'

He raised a brow at her sarcasm.

'What?' she demanded. 'That's what you want to hear, isn't it? Take some of the guilt away.'

'I don't feel any guilt about leaving her with my mother.' It was one of the only things he *could* think about without feeling as if a heavy weight were slowly crushing his insides.

'Well, you should.'

If he hadn't recognised her belligerence as a mask, he would have left her to stew. Except her hands were trembling and she was blinking too rapidly to be doing anything other than fighting tears.

As much as he hated her, witnessing her trying so hard not to cry tore something in him.

Stepping over, he sat on the bed next to her and took her hand. It was cold.

'I don't feel any guilt because I know my mother will take the utmost care of her. Lily will be spoiled rotten—if she wants caviar in her milk I promise my mother will provide it.'

The tiniest hint of a smile played on the corners of her lips. 'I know. I know. It's just…'

He waited for her to continue. 'It's just what?'

She pulled her hand away and gazed at Lily. It hadn't escaped his attention that, apart from her initial glare, she refused to look at him.

'Florence is so far away.' She sighed. 'Maybe it would be easier if the party was in Lebbrossi or Palermo; places we can nip back from quickly if anything were to happen…'

'Nothing is going to happen.'

'It might.'

'Grace, look at me.' When she kept her focus on Lily he repeated his command, catching her chin with a finger and forcing her attention. Her hazel eyes were bright with unshed tears. 'I'll arrange things with the aviation authorities in Florence so that, in the case of an emergency, we can take the jet back to Palermo at any time necessary.'

'Can you do that?'

'Yes.'

'But if we're flying from the main airport, aren't we supposed to select an advance time slot and—?'

'I'll fix it. It will not be a problem.'

She continued to look at him dubiously.

'Does this solution not ease your mind?'

'Only if you promise not to use intimidation or violence to get your own way.'

He should be affronted that she would think such a thing of him. Yet he could not blame her. Grace was the sort of person who would rather rescue a bug than kill it. Any form of violence was alien to her way of thinking—even if he went through everything about his business ventures and partnership in detail, and explained why things were the way they were, she would never understand. He'd known that from the start, within days of buying into that first casino, when the first man had been foolish enough to steal from it and Francesco's men had been set upon him. He'd known Grace would never accept it or understand the necessity behind it.

There were times he struggled to accept and understand it himself. There had been many a time when only the stiffest of Scotches had allowed him to blur the images that played behind his retinas and dulled the nausea that lined his stomach.

Rubbing his thumb along her soft cheek, he said, 'The only asset I will use to get my own way will be of a monetary value.'

'You can afford it,' she said with what could almost be called a smile.

There was nothing he could say to that. He could afford anything his heart desired. *Apart from Grace's heart*, the sly voice came back at him.

In the beat of a second his head began to pound with the sound of a thousand drums.

Her eyes held his, a softness in them he hadn't seen for so long he had forgotten how amazing it felt to be on the receiving end of it. The hazel in them melted and darkened while her lips parted. Her chest rose and fell sharply, colour heightening her complexion as she held the gaze binding them together.

Dio, but if she wasn't the most beautiful woman on the planet. Was it any wonder he was having such trouble finding another woman to hold his interest for longer than the blink of an eye when he had married the most desirable of them all? Her small breasts jutted through the tight green cashmere sweater she wore. Unthinking, he raised the hand not stroking her cheek and cupped one, sucking in a breath as an enormous jolt surged through him.

Her eyes widened, her own shallow breaths hitching. She raised a hand in turn and brought it to his face where it hovered, not quite touching him, before a pained, almost desperate look crossed her features.

She blinked and shook her head, the softness and desire gone, replaced with the hard wariness he was becoming far too accustomed to. Her full lips, which for a few brief moments he had been about to shape his mouth against and plunder the hot sweetness within, tightened.

She turned away and got to her feet. 'Can you leave us now? Lily needs a bath and I need to write a list for your mum.'

He stared from his wife to his daughter, his head pounding, his heart aching with as much force as the throbbing between his legs. 'Can I bathe her?'

She twisted her head to look back at him. 'You?'

'I've missed so much of her life.' For once there was no accusation in either his tone or his meaning. 'I meant what I said before. I want to be a proper father to her.'

He was certain she would refuse. And when she did? Then he would accept her decision. Grace was Lily's mother. He'd made half her DNA but he would have to earn the right to be her father.

To his surprise, she inclined her head, a wry smile forming on her lips. 'If I were you, I would change into something more waterproof. She has a tendency to splash.'

'I'm sure I'll be fine.'

Twenty minutes later, he regretted not taking Grace's advice. He would never have believed someone so small could make so much mess. Lily's plump legs had kicked most of the water out of the baby bath. The floor was soaked. He was drenched, his bespoke trousers ruined.

When Grace poked her head round the bathroom door she did nothing to hide her smirk before disappearing again.

Unlike the night before, when he'd had Lily sleep with him and a lack of proper winding on his part—or so he had learned from his mother when he confessed the incident to her earlier—had made her throw up, he had little trouble putting her nappy on and dressing her. This time it only took three attempts before he was satisfied the fiddly poppers of the romper suit were properly done up.

Only when Lily was settled in her cot, her belly full and properly winded by Grace, did he leave them.

He shut the door and expelled a long breath, taken aback at the physical wrench leaving them caused.

Putting his daughter to bed, his wife by his side...something inside him had shifted. He couldn't pinpoint what, exactly, but he knew he needed to speak to Pepe before he and Grace flew to Florence the next day. He also knew his scheduled meeting with Francesco Calvetti before the party would have a different agenda from the one Francesco was expecting.

CHAPTER NINE

THE HOTEL THEY checked into dated back to the Renaissance and was as grand as any they had stayed in before. With its high frescoed ceilings and intricate architecture, it was the sort of place Grace loved to explore in detail.

Today, though, the last thing on her mind was exploration of any kind. Being such a distance from Lily felt as if her heart had been ripped out. For twelve long weeks it had been just the two of them, but, while the bond between them had been strong from the word go, she had always been aware of something missing, something she hadn't dared put a name to. She still wouldn't put a name to it, too mindful of the danger it could bring if voiced, even if only in her own head.

That missing something…it had vanished the day they had been forced to move back to Sicily and back into Luca's world.

She tried to tell herself the nausea within her belly was due to separation anxiety and nothing else.

It had nothing to do with being alone with Luca—properly alone—for the first time in so, so long.

But something had changed. She could feel it. Loathing was no longer the chief emotion binding them together. It was more than just desire too, although yesterday, sitting on that bed with him cupping her breast, the heat from his hand permeating the fabric of her top…

They had both been fighting to contain the desire that leaped from one to the other, almost as if the charge that lived within her plugged into a charge within him.

She'd had to fight with everything in her not to press her chest into his palm. She'd had to fight not to touch his face, not to rub her cheek against his, not to simply jump onto his lap, smother him with craven kisses and…

She shuddered and closed her eyes.

If Lily hadn't been in the room with them, she had no idea if she would have been strong enough to keep the war within herself going.

However much she wanted to deny it, anticipation brewed within her too. That treacherous charge in her stomach flamed brightly.

It was at times like this she could punch herself. *She* was in control of her body and its reactions. She and she alone.

To take her mind off her strangely melancholic mood and thoughts, she opened the wardrobe door and stared, not for the first time, at the hideous dress. If there were a bottle of red wine to hand she would happily tip it all over the vile creation. For good measure she would splosh the dregs all over the foul beige shoes Luca had selected for her to wear with it. Her dowdy old primary school teacher had worn similar shoes. However, looking at them cheered her up a little; right then she needed physical evidence of her husband's bastard tendencies.

Checking her watch for the umpteenth time, she saw she still had well over an hour to kill before they were due to leave. Luca had disappeared to a meeting within minutes of their arrival saying only that he would be back in time to shower and change. She hadn't asked who the meeting was with—who else could it be but Francesco? Still, for all she knew, he could be overseeing the beating of another hapless fool stupid enough to try to cheat Luca Mastrangelo and associates.

He hadn't always been like this. The first year of their marriage—although restrictive in terms of freedom—had in all other respects been perfect. Luca had been perfect.

The change had been so subtle she had hardly noticed it, not at first. As his evenings away from her had increased from the odd one here and there to almost every other, she'd comforted herself knowing that more often than not he would join her in the early hours, whether in the master bedroom or the smaller bedroom in her studio. By the last few months of their marriage, those evenings when he was around, instead of the coffee they usually used as fuel, he would have a Scotch in hand. His temper had shortened too—not against her, apart from that one time in his office, but she had been acutely aware of how tense he was, the sharpness of his tone. She'd been desperate for him to confide his troubles in her. But he'd refused. He'd refused to even acknowledge there was anything wrong.

Looking back, she could see she'd never pushed him that hard for answers. Apart from the row they'd had the day before she left him, she'd never *really* pushed him, and even then she'd backed down.

It had been far easier to bury her head in the sand and pretend everything was all right.

And was that what Luca had been doing—*was* doing—too? Burying his head in the sand?

The more she thought about it, the more confused she felt. His abhorrence at being labelled a gangster was real. He genuinely didn't see himself with those eyes.

Closing the wardrobe door, she debated calling Donatella again and checking that Lily was okay. Before she could dial the number, a message pinged into her phone. Opening it, she felt her heart lighten to see a photo of Lily lying on the sofa in her usual starfish position, beaming her new gummy smile. The picture had also been sent to Luca.

The accompanying message read:

Lily sends you both big kisses and says she wants you both to stop worrying and enjoy your night away.

Grace bit her lip and brushed away a relieved tear.

God, she was being such a sap. She wasn't the first woman to leave her baby and she wouldn't be the last. Lily was being cared for by someone who loved her deeply and wouldn't harm a hair on her head.

She reread the message. The *both* part of it jumped out. Did that mean Luca had been calling his mum too?

Watching him bathe and dress their daughter had been so funny and so very touching. When she had got up that morning to give Lily her early bottle, he had appeared within minutes and chivvied Grace back to bed, insisting on feeding Lily himself.

Dear Lord, but he had fallen in love with Lily. She could see it in the softness of his eyes and the gentle tone of his voice, the tender way he held her. Their little daughter had crawled into his heart.

Donatella was smitten too.

If she found a way to escape, how could she, in all conscience, take Lily and disappear? It would be kinder to rip their hearts out and stamp on them.

But she could not allow herself to think of these things. She needed to concentrate on shoring up her mental defences against her husband. She had a whole evening to get through, during which she would be expected to act as Luca's good Sicilian wife and pretend to be some obedient creature whose only objective in life was to please her husband. She would have to pretend she still loved him, pretend she enjoyed having her hand held in his.

Most of all she would have to convince herself he meant nothing to her, that her blood didn't heat or her pulse rocket when he touched her.

Her fingers began to itch, a feeling that startled her. It wasn't the same itch as when she'd wanted to slap him. This was an itch from old.

For the first time in almost a year she felt a desperate urge to paint, to draw, to sketch.

Before she could begin tearing the suite apart looking for some paper and a pen or pencil—when, she wondered, had she stopped carrying a sketch pad with her everywhere she went?—there was a light rap on the suite door.

She checked the spyhole, only opening the door when satisfied her visitor was a member of the hotel staff.

'Signora Mastrangelo?' the severe-looking woman asked, a large package in her hands.

'Sì,' Grace replied, showing off a little of her Italian.

'This has just arrived for you,' the woman said in perfect English.

'Who's it from?'

'I do not know, *signora*. Maybe there is a note inside for you?' she added helpfully.

'Thank you. I mean, *grazie*.'

'Prego.'

Grace closed the door and took the box to the dining table, intrigued and a little wary of what could be inside and who could have sent it.

Clenching her teeth together, she took a deep breath and ripped off the brown packaging. Inside was a long cream box with a familiar motif.

Her heart suddenly wedged in her throat, she opened

the lid as if she were expecting a load of cobras and rattlesnakes to be inside.

Her hands flew to her mouth. No note accompanied it. No note needed to accompany it.

Inside was the peacock-skirted dress she had fallen in love with before Luca had forced the beige monstrosity on her.

He must have noticed her staring at it on the mannequin. Not only had he noticed but he had remembered.

If her belly wasn't already a mass of noodles and butterflies before, it was now a riot to match the beautiful colours of her dress.

When had he bought it? And why? Why now? So many confused thoughts were flying through her head that at first she didn't hear the new rap on the suite door.

Opening it, she found the same employee standing at the threshold, this time holding another, smaller package.

'My apologies, *signora*. I had not been informed that this too was delivered by the courier.'

Less than a minute later, Grace opened the package and discovered the most amazing pair of high, strappy gold sandals.

Grace was applying her make-up when she heard Luca enter the suite. Immediately her steady hand began to shake, violently enough for her to stab herself in the eye with her mascara wand.

'Grace?' he called out.

'I'm in my room,' she replied, putting a palm to her smarting eye.

'Are you ready?'

'Nearly.'

'Will you be ready to leave in fifteen minutes?'

'Yes.'

Ready in fifteen minutes? Never mind that she needed to reapply her make-up and change from the hotel robe into the dress, she could have fifteen years and she doubted she would be ready.

'Are you all right in there?' He must have heard something in her voice because his tone was concerned.

'I'm fine.'

Removing her palm, she almost laughed out loud at her reflection. One eye was still perfectly made up. The other, the one she had stabbed, had all the make-up running, the eye itself bright red and weeping.

'Brilliant,' she muttered under her breath.

Her door opened.

'You're not fine,' Luca accused, strolling over and peering closely at her. 'What have you done?'

'Stabbed myself with my mascara. Don't worry. I'll give it a couple of minutes to stop weeping and then I'll redo it.'

A slow grin spread over his face. 'You look like Morticia Addams.'

'Very funny.'

'Or that clown. What's its name? Poirot?'

'Pierrot,' she corrected with a snigger.

'That's the one. You painted your friend Cara as Pierrot once.'

'So I did.' She grinned, remembering. Luca had belly-laughed when he'd seen the finished product. 'It was revenge after she trashed one of my dresses when she'd drunk too much wine.'

'Was that when we'd been out to that party in Palermo and she tripped over a tree?'

'Yep.' Taking a quick peek in the mirror, she grimaced. 'I look a mess.'

'How did you come to assault yourself with your make-up?'

'It's all your fault,' she said, fixing him with a stern look. 'You startled me when you started barging around the suite like a jumbo elephant.'

'I'm nothing like a jumbo elephant.' He raised a brow. 'Apart from one particular part of my anatomy.'

She raised a brow in turn and indicated the door. 'Shouldn't you be going for a shower?'

'Wouldn't you prefer to discuss my jumbo-sized appendage?'

A warm, bubbly feeling spread through her veins. She slapped his arm lightly. 'Your modesty never fails to astound me. Now go and have a shower before you stink the whole suite out.'

'I'm going, I'm going,' he said with mock surrender. When he reached the door, he turned back to her. 'Did you receive any packages while I was at my meeting?'

And just like that, she remembered where she was, and all the good feelings inside her vanished.

Consternation hit.

For a few brief seconds, time had turned and transplanted her—them—into the past.

The here and now had disappeared. For that brief moment in time when they had teased each other she had forgotten that she hated him.

'Yes. I received them. Thank you.' And shortly she would have to put on the dress and shoes. Call her contrary but part of her would prefer to wear the hideous beige creation. At least then she would be able to seethe at him all night, would be in no danger of further softening.

When he left, she went straight to the bathroom and washed her face. She was patting it dry when Luca came back into her room.

'Here, take this,' he said, handing her a small tube. 'Put

a couple of drops in your eye and it should get rid of the redness.'

Don't be touched at his thoughtfulness, she warned herself. *Keep your guard up.*

He stood, watching her, waiting for her to say something.

'Thanks.'

He nodded. 'No problem. I've told the driver we'll be a few minutes late, so don't rush.'

'I wouldn't dream of it. I'm sure the last thing you want is for your perfect wife to look as if she was thrown together.'

His mouth tightened. 'That's not what I meant and you know it. I was thinking of you. If you want to twist it then that's your problem.'

Grace stared at his retreating figure wishing she could take it back.

But take what back? Luca had been very clear in his expectation that she be a good Sicilian wife and nothing had been said to alter that.

They couldn't live in a permanent state of angst. It was natural some of the good feeling from their previous marital incarnation should seep into the fabric of this new form. She just had to be alert and ready for it.

She could not afford to drop her guard. Not for a second.

When Luca left his room twenty minutes later, he found Grace sitting on the sofa with her back to him, a glass of red wine on the table in front of her.

'You were quick,' he commented, helping himself to the glass and opened bottle she had left out for him.

She got to her feet and reached for her wine. Taking a sip of it, she turned to face him.

He took her in slowly, studying every inch.

That his wife had never been one for spending hours

on her appearance was somewhat of an understatement. Considering she spent—or *had* spent—most of her natural state splattered with paint, she always used to joke it was pointless. However, she had adored dressing up for nights out, could transform her fresh-faced beauty into gorgeous, quirky sophistication with nothing more than a tiny make-up bag of tricks.

Tonight, in fifteen short minutes, she had outdone herself.

'You're beautiful,' he said hoarsely, unable to take his eyes off her. The sunny colours were perfect on her, the buttercup bodice enhancing her small cleavage and the litheness of her stature. The front of the dress rested above her knees, displaying her long, slender legs to perfection, the back of it mere inches from the floor. Her hair, which had grown into a very short bob, had been spiked in all directions, her make-up bold, her eyes painted a smoky brown that darkened the hazel of her eyes. A splash of orange lipstick, that on any other woman would look crass, completed the look to perfection.

He watched as she swallowed and moved towards him, the peacock skirt swaying as she walked.

'Could you do the zip up for me, please?' Her voice was terse, her features hard.

'Of course.'

In her room, for all of a minute, he'd thought he had found his old Grace, the woman whose mocking was never malicious, intended only to amuse, never to sting.

This woman before him was not that Grace.

He wanted to find his old Grace again. She was in there, somewhere. He wanted to reach in and pull her out permanently.

She turned her back to him. She'd managed to zip it three quarters of the way up. He imagined her fighting it, contorting herself into all different positions in an attempt to zip it fully, anything rather than have to ask him for help.

Standing closer than was necessary, close enough to hear the shallowness of her breaths, he placed a hand on her shoulder, bare except for the thin strap of her dress. Her skin held none of the ruddiness her compatriots were famed for. Grace's skin was a light honey tone and satin to the touch.

He pulled the zip up to where it ended just below her shoulder blades. Instead of stopping and stepping back, he trailed his fingers along that soft skin to the base of her neck.

She stood rigid, like the very mannequin that had worn this same dress, no longer breathing. He brushed his hands down her long, supple arms then snaked them around her waist and pressed against her. She would have to be a corpse not to feel the length of his hardness.

'What are you doing?' she rasped, stepping out of his hold.

'Enjoying my wife.'

'You buy me a dress you know I like and think you can *enjoy* me?'

'Stop twisting things.' He raked his fingers through his freshly styled hair, uncaring that he mussed it. Every time he took a step forward she jumped a mile back.

'Then why did you buy it? What happened to me wearing the punishment dress? Did you buy this as a way of softening me up so I'd fall into bed with you? Or was it an attack of the guilts?'

'I do not need to soften you up to get you back into my bed.' Ignoring her mention of guilt, he took in her heightened colour, the anger in her eyes that fought with the desire also residing there. 'All I would have to do is kiss you and you would be begging for me to take you.'

'Bull—'

'Would you like to put it to the test?' he interrupted. 'One kiss and see where it leads, see whether it leads to you begging for more?'

She fixed her hazel eyes on him, her throat working frantically. 'It'll be a cold day in hell before I kiss you or go anywhere near a bed with you in it.'

'If being in hell means sharing a bed with you, I'll take that over heaven.'

Her mouth formed a perfect 'O' before she snapped it shut and grabbed her clutch bag from the bureau. 'Shouldn't we be making a move?'

'Yes, my good Sicilian wife,' he agreed, fighting to keep his tone amiable. Tonight would likely be awkward enough for them both—he wanted her to at least relax enough to enjoy some of it, but, by God, she was making it hard.

He extended his arm to her. 'It is time for us to be sociable and party with Florence's finest.'

'If they're friends of yours, I expect the party will be full of gangsters with guns.'

The good humour he had been clinging on to by the skin of his teeth vanished, her testiness clearly contagious. 'You push my tolerance too far. I might want you back in my bed, *bella*, but do not think it means I am disregarding our agreement. If you want to stay in Lily's life you had damn well better behave yourself tonight.'

As they were in Florence, in Grace's eyes the art capital of the world, she expected the party to be a refined affair with soft background music and plenty of canapés. And a few machine guns discreetly tucked away in full view.

Francesco Calvetti's party was located in his new hotel, which was as opulent and plush as the hotel she and Luca were staying in, and seeped with as much architectural history. Yet she could give it only cursory appreciation, her exchange with Luca leaving her feeling all wrung out. It was so *hard* having to keep up the fight of her responses towards him. When it came to Luca, her head and her body were poles apart. It was a fight she feared her body was winning.

The drive to the hotel had been a game in ignoring each other: Grace looking out of her window, Luca emailing and conducting whatever cyber business was necessary on a Saturday evening.

However hard she ignored him, her body remained painfully aware.

They entered the lobby flanked by four bodyguards. Luca hooked a muscular arm around her waist. 'Smile and act happy,' he said into her ear, the menacing undertow audible.

She responded with a smile of such saccharine goodness she hoped the sweetness made him puke. Anything had to be better than him knowing her whole body vibrated with excitement at his closeness.

It was somewhat of a shock when they entered the ballroom and found it transformed into a nightclub. Or that was what she assumed it had been turned into with the heavy velvet drapes that covered the walls and the dark mood lighting. Loud music pumped, not the quaint string group she had envisaged but a DJ in a booth high up on a stage, already surrounded by a throng of beautiful women. She recognised him as the house DJ employed at Luca and Francesco's nightclub in Palermo. She had visited it twice and loathed it. Luca had holed himself up in the offices, leaving her bored out of her skull. At least when she accompanied him to one of the casinos there was always something to do that didn't involve gyrating into strangers' groins.

She could feel the vibrations through her fantastic gold sandals. Next to the DJ's booth were two caged podiums in which semi-naked lap dancers writhed. Much as it made her feminist hackles rise, even she could see the professional pride they took in their performances.

For the second time that evening she wished she had her sketchbook with her.

The ballroom was packed, not with shady men in black—although there were a fair number of them around—but men and women from the height of Sicilian and Italian society, minor British royalty and American film and rock stars. She even recognised a few patrons of the arts. Dotted around the enormous room were enough armed guards—unobtrusive but to her trained eye obvious—to overthrow a government.

It seemed as if Luca knew all the guests. Forced to stick to his side, she was introduced to dozens of both new and familiar faces, all of whom studied her with great interest. It was the familiar faces she found the hardest to endure, the curiosity in their eyes at the return of the prodigal wife.

She'd had no idea anyone would be interested about the state of their marriage, not at a birthday party in Florence.

Luca must have picked up on the curiosity too, for he kept her hand tightly clasped in his. Or was he simply marking his territory?

Glasses of champagne were thrust into her free hand, which she took cautious sips of, careful not to drink too much. Alcohol had a terrible habit of loosening her inhibitions and she needed to keep them tightly squashed away.

Her hackles rose again when a tall, lithe man approached them, two women walking to heel as if especially trained.

Francesco Calvetti. The party boy. Luca's main business associate.

CHAPTER TEN

DRESSED IN A dapper silver suit and open-necked black shirt, and looking as if he had just stepped off a catwalk, Francesco was sinisterly handsome. Grace would have bet every penny she owned he winked at his own reflection whenever he looked in a mirror. She had met him half a dozen times and he never failed to make her skin crawl. If she were to paint him she would cast him as a vulture.

'Luca!' He opened his arms wide and pulled him into an embrace that involved lots of back-slapping.

Grace watched Luca carefully, certain she had felt him tense at Francesco's approach. He responded with the same masculine enthusiasm, but as they conversed she could hear the tension in his voice, even if she couldn't understand the words.

Finally, Luca switched to English. 'Do you remember my wife, Grace?'

'But of course.' Francesco's English was faultless. He took her hand and pressed a kiss to it. There was nothing seedy in his manner but, for reasons she could not even begin to quantify, she wanted to snatch her hand away and disinfect it.

'I trust you have fully recovered from the ailment that kept you away for so long?' From the tone of his voice, he seemed to be speaking in code. Unfortunately she did not have the faintest idea what the code stood for.

'Yes, she is fully recovered,' Luca interjected smoothly.

'Excellent news. Please, both of you, accept my congratulations on the birth of your first child together. I hope your family is blessed with many more *bambini*.'

'That's what we hope for too,' said Luca.

The conversation ended with the men exchanging another back-breaking embrace before Francesco disappeared into a melee of beautiful women.

'What the hell was that about?' Grace demanded. 'What am I supposed to have recovered from?'

'Pre-natal depression.'

'What?'

'I told him you'd been in England.' Here he shrugged. 'His own mother suffered from severe pre-natal depression. He assumed you had suffered from it too and had gone to England to be cared for by your mother.'

'Why didn't you set him straight?' she seethed. 'Why couldn't you say I left you but that we had decided to try again for Lily's sake?'

He quelled her with a stare. 'Absolutely not.'

'Of course not,' she said sarcastically. She could feel her skin heating, his implacability heightening her anger. 'It would never do for people to think there was something wrong with *you* that made me leave, would there?'

'There is *nothing* wrong with me.' His eyes bored into her. If Grace's temperature had risen, his had lifted in conjunction. 'All that's wrong is how you interpreted matters to suit your own notions of how a businessman is supposed to conduct his affairs.'

If only she had been born with Medusa-like powers she could turn him into stone to match his heart.

'Where are you going?' he snapped as she stepped away.

'To the ladies', before I give in to temptation and cause a scene. Why? Are you going to follow me to make sure I don't escape?'

A pulse in his jaw throbbed as he leaned into her, his breath hot against her ear. 'If you want to leave, then I promise you one thing: I will not stop you and I will not look for you.'

'I think you'll find that was two things.'

Leaving him to stew in a pit of his own self-righteous anger, Grace proceeded to the ladies' cloakroom, concentrating only on putting one foot in front of another.

In the sanctuary of the opulent bathroom, she took stock of her appearance. As she retouched her eyeliner and reapplied her lipstick all she could think was her own husband had let Francesco think she suffered from depression.

The worst of it was, she could actually understand why a man with Luca's ferocious pride would allow such a thing. In a mad kind of way, it made a heck of a lot of sense. His wife had vanished from the face of the earth. She hadn't just left him, she'd disappeared without a trace. When eventually he found her and discovered she'd had his child, what was he supposed to tell people? That his own wife thought him so evil she would hide his flesh and blood from him? Honour and pride were everything, and she had wounded both.

By letting people believe she had left out of something beyond either of their control he could save face. For both of them.

Jeez, she was actually making excuses for him.

Only when she was satisfied her emotions were sufficiently masked did she leave the bathroom.

The ballroom had become so crowded she had trouble finding him. Snaking her way through the mass of bodies, she finally spotted him on a stool at the bar, nursing a glass of champagne.

As she neared him a warm hand grabbed her wrist. 'There you are. I thought you'd run away again.'

Twisting round, she met the contempt that was in her brother-in-law's eyes. 'Pepe! I didn't know you were here.'

'Well, I am.'

She attempted a smile. She had always adored Pepe, a man who gave the air that life was just one big party. Apart from when arguing with his brother, of course. Not tonight though. Tonight he looked darkly serious.

'Your mother said you would be home a few days ago. Have you been avoiding me?'

He sighed, checked over his shoulder to where Luca was sitting and tugged her into an alcove, away from the throng of people moving like a river around them. 'I thought it best to keep my distance until I could be certain I wouldn't throttle you for what you put my brother through. I didn't think he would appreciate that.'

'He would have cheered you on.'

His eyes became mocking. 'Why would that be?'

'He hates me.' Whatever Luca might say to strangers to explain her absence, his brother would get the truth. However divergent their lives and personalities, however ferocious their arguments, they were close.

'You stole his baby from him.' He made it sound so simple.

She sighed. 'I wish it were as straightforward as that.'

'It is. You ran away and stole his baby, ergo he hated you.'

It was Grace's turn to look over her shoulder, barely registering the past tense Pepe had just used. A woman had joined Luca at the bar. Whatever he'd said to her must have been the funniest thing in the world, for she threw her head back and laughed.

Pepe followed her line of sight. 'Worried he's searching for your replacement?'

She rolled her eyes, masking the stabbing pain piercing her heart. 'I have no control over what Luca does.'

'You have *no idea.*' He shook his head with a scowl of incredulity. 'Do you have any idea why I'm here at this scumbag's party?'

Her brow furrowed. 'Do you mean Francesco?'

'Who else? I'm here because I don't trust the bastard. Now that Luca is cutting all ties with him—'

Certain she had misheard, she cut him off. 'He's what?'

'Luca is ending their association. He told him at their meeting earlier.' His eyes narrowed as he took in her shock. 'I assumed he'd told you.'

She shook her head, hundreds of thoughts fighting for space in her head. 'Luca stopped discussing business with me a long time ago. Were you never part of their business dealings?'

His face contorted into something ugly. 'Francesco Calvetti is scum. I would sooner have made a deal with the devil. The terms would have been friendlier.'

'So you're only here to watch Luca's back?'

'Why else?'

Luca had cut his ties with Francesco...?

She remembered the look on Francesco's face at the casino, when he and Luca had been interrogating that poor man. What she remembered from that brief moment she had been in the office, before Luca had frogmarched her out, had been the cold cruelty she'd observed in Francesco's eyes. It had been in marked contrast to the thoughtfulness she had seen in her husband's.

Francesco enjoyed using threats and violence, whereas

Luca used them only because he felt it necessary. There was a big difference.

It shouldn't make any difference to how she felt about him, but it did.

'I need to get back to Luca,' she murmured, her eyes fixed on her husband and the buxom woman jabbering away in his ear.

As she made to walk off, Pepe called after her, 'Have you seen your friend since you returned?'

'Who? Cara?'

He nodded. His position and the angle of the light above him highlighted the silvery scar that ran across his left cheek.

'Not yet.' Cara's continued elusiveness concerned her. It was unlike her tender-hearted friend to be so evasive…

A thought occurred to her.

'Was it you who stole the data from her phone?'

He cast his eyes about, looking anywhere but at her.

Jaw clenched, she shook her head. It was inconceivable Cara would have let Luca within ten miles of her, but Pepe…

'Cara is the sweetest, nicest person in the world. If you've hurt her, I swear I'll make you live to regret it.'

With a parting 'You don't know what you're talking about,' Pepe disappeared into the crowd of revellers.

Grace took a deep breath to clear her head. Right now, she would have to put her friend to the back of her mind. As selfish as she knew it to be, she had more pressing worries to deal with.

She headed back into the throng and wove her way towards Luca. She could not quite hide the fear that Pepe's analysis was accurate. Was Luca still holding interviews for the role of his mistress?

Judging by the way the woman at the bar was leaning into him, it appeared so.

As she closed in on him her stomach roiled.

Watching her husband flirt with other women was surreal. First the assistant in the boutique and now this tanned, pneumatically boobed creature.

When they had been married—properly married, that was—she had often noticed women eye him up but that had been the extent of their interest. She and Luca had been practically glued at the hip. If another woman had tried to garner his attention he wouldn't have noticed or cared.

As she drew closer she realised any flirting was one-sided, a feeling confirmed when he looked up and she saw the dullness in his eyes.

That look made her heart lighten and relief spread its tentacles through her. The woman could be flirting with a brick wall for all the attention Luca was paying her.

Deliberately, she stepped between them.

'Excuse me!' The woman spoke with a broad cockney accent. Able to look closely at her, Grace recognised her as a glamour model, a favourite of the British press.

'I'm sorry,' she said lightly. 'That was incredibly rude of me. I'm Grace, Luca's wife.' A glass of champagne had been placed on the bar. Without missing a beat, she picked it up and downed it.

'Oi. That was mine.'

'Really?' She feigned ignorance. 'I do apologise. I thought Luca had ordered it for me. Please, let me get you another one.'

'No, don't bother.' The model pursed her lips together and stuck her clutch bag under her arm.

'Lovely to meet you,' Grace called as the model sashayed off to the dance floor, where a whole heap of rich men were congregated.

Luca stared at her, his lips twitching, before raising his chin and taking a swig of his champagne. 'Marking your territory?'

'You should be thanking me for getting rid of her.' Her fake bonhomie faded away. She had to ask, 'Unless you were auditioning her for the role of your mistress?'

His gaze didn't waver. 'I don't want a mistress.'

Something hot flooded her veins and seeped through her bones and into every inch of her flesh. Her lips parted, but no sound came out.

The icy darkness in his eyes melted. It took everything she had to wrench her eyes from his heated gaze.

She swallowed and stared at his champagne flute before being drawn back to meet his eyes. 'I thought you only drank Scotch nowadays?'

He didn't so much as flicker. 'When I realised that you weren't dead and had simply run away, I stopped drinking. I needed every wit I had trying to find you.'

'So my leaving did *some* good.' She smiled to cover the sting that lashed across her chest. As much as she knew he'd deserved every second of worry, it hurt her heart to think of the pain she had put him through. 'I was starting to worry for your liver.'

'You had nothing to worry about.'

'Didn't I?' she asked pointedly.

From the flicker in his eyes, he knew as well as she that she was not just referring to his drinking habits.

'I saw you talking with Pepe,' he said, blatantly changing the subject. 'I'm pleased he didn't give in to his impulse of strangling you.'

'So am I. I think he's saving all his hatred for when he gets the opportunity to dismember Francesco.'

Mirth played on his firm lips. Turning his head, Luca

caught the bartender's eye and indicated for more champagne.

'Francesco is not the demon Pepe would have you believe.' He paused. 'Well, maybe a little.'

'He told me you were cutting your business ties with him.'

'That is correct.'

'Why?'

'That is not a conversation for now.'

'Then when? Tonight? Tomorrow? Next year?'

He turned back to her. 'Tonight.'

'Promise?'

'I give you my word.'

She bit her lip, wishing she could read his mind.

A strange flicker crossed his face. 'I'm sorry I let Francesco believe you had pre-natal depression.'

An apology? From Luca? That had to be a first.

'It was the truth,' she admitted, expelling a huge lungful of air.

He raised an eyebrow, a furrow running down his forehead.

She smiled wryly. 'Oh, it wasn't serious like you told him. More a constant lethargy. Motivating myself to keep moving on kept getting harder.' As if her tongue had a mind of its own, she confided the darkness she had, at the time, been too scared to properly acknowledge to herself. 'It got worse after Lily was born. That's why I bought all the exercise equipment—I was terrified of being put on anti-depressants, terrified of failing Lily. I'd read exercise was a good method of combating it.'

'Did it work?'

'A little.' She shrugged, realising for the first time that her return to Sicily—to Luca—had coincided with the return of her old energy levels. For sure, she was still tired—

having a small baby who rarely slept through the night ensured that—but the cold fog that had enveloped her bones had vanished. 'I definitely feel better in myself now.'

'That's good.' He paused. 'I'm sorry I wasn't there to support you.'

It was on the tip of her tongue to say the same in return, but this time, by the slightest of threads, she managed to keep her mouth shut. To utter another word would be madness. She was in enough danger as it was.

Fresh flutes of champagne were placed before them. Luca handed one to Grace and held his own aloft. His eyes flashed. *'Salute.'*

'Salute,' she echoed, chinking her flute to his. She took a long sip and closed her eyes, enjoying the taste and the sensation of bubbles fizzing in her mouth. It was much the same way she used to fizz at Luca's touch. The way she still did…

'We should dance,' he said.

She took a deep breath and opened her eyes to meet his gaze. 'Why? So we can convince everyone here that we're happy together?'

'Because I want to dance with the sexiest woman here and show them she's mine.'

She swallowed away the dryness of her throat. 'I'm not yours. Only in name.' Even as she spoke the words she knew them to be a lie. Luca had imprinted himself indelibly into every one of her senses.

He leaned into her and spoke into her neck. 'You will *always* be mine.'

The warmth of his breath sent tiny pulsations darting through her. She swayed, her heels no protection against the dizziness evoked by his touch.

He covered her hand, lacing his fingers through hers.

He felt so warm, his touch penetrating her skin and dancing into the very fabric of her being.

As if acting of its own accord, her other hand came to rest on his shoulder.

His muscles bunched beneath her touch. She felt the potent strength that ran through his being, a strength she had always taken such comfort from.

The stars that resided in the midnight of his eyes gleamed, holding her gaze, trapping her into their depths. He had shaved before they left their hotel yet dark stubble had already broken out along his jawline. If there was a sexier man in the world she had yet to meet him.

He brushed his lips against her neck, nipping at the sensitive skin. 'Dance with me.'

She wanted to, badly. She wanted to say to hell with the past and to hell with the future, to simply take the moment for what it was.

His hand sidled down her chest, tracing the outline of her breast, coming to rest on her hip. He dug his fingers through the soft fabric and into her flesh, and pulled her so she was flat against him. 'Dance with me,' he repeated.

For the first time since she'd left Sicily, Grace felt as if the essence of herself had slipped out of the recess in which it had been hiding.

Luca was like a drug to her. She could survive without him but it was like breathing air with only a fraction of the usual oxygen.

She hated him.

She loved him.

The two sides were interchangeable.

The only constant she felt was desire. And she was sick of fighting it and pushing it away. There could only ever be one outcome.

Bending her head, she caught the top of his ear between her teeth. ‘Yes,’ she breathed, tracing her tongue across the contours. ‘I’ll dance with you.’

CHAPTER ELEVEN

THE DANCE FLOOR heaved with bodies, the music blasting out an R & B mix with a sensuous beat that throbbed through the wooden floorboards. The model who had flirted with Luca and whose name already escaped him was grinding with a member of the British aristocracy.

And he was dancing with his wife, a leg pressed between hers as they swayed together in time to the pulsating music, her face buried in his neck, her breath warm on his skin.

She moulded into him perfectly. Just as she always had.

This was an event he had looked at as a necessary evil, even before he had decided to cut all business association with Francesco Calvetti. After their meeting that day, attendance had been a requirement to show the world they were parting on good terms. The last thing either man needed was any usurper sniffing around trying to detect weakness.

The subtle politics of his business life was enough to give anyone a headache.

Grace eased his headache. Holding her in his arms drove away the demons that resided within him, just as it always had. No matter how out of control he had felt at times, one embrace from his wife had always been enough to temper it, if only a fraction.

For the moment he could almost forget the demons she had placed in there.

If he closed his eyes, he could almost believe the past year or so had never occurred. Physically they were as in tune as if they had never been apart.

Slowly he ran his hands down the length of her back until he reached her bottom. Cupping her buttocks, he pressed her ever closer. She could be left in no doubt of his arousal. And why would either of them doubt it? Physically, they were made for each other.

His quest to find a mistress had ended before it started. He had to get used to the fact there was not a woman alive, other than his wife, who did anything for him.

Before Grace had exploded into his life with all the subtlety of a flying brick, he'd never been so selective. His body had never been so stubborn to respond.

He shivered as her fingers brushed the nape of his neck. Such clever, talented fingers.

When had she last painted? In the Cornish cottage where he had found her, there had been none of the usual paraphernalia that used to accompany her everywhere. There had been no sign she had picked up a paintbrush or even a simple pencil since she had left him. The thought saddened him. The thought that he could be responsible for it made his chest tighten.

She raised her thigh slightly and ground against him, nipping at his neck. All his thoughts turned to fog, her soft lips sending darts of pleasure pulsing through his blood.

Turning his head, he captured her mouth in his and closed his eyes. Her hot sweetness engulfed his senses.

He forgot to breathe.

There it was, the taste that filled his mouth with moisture, the heat that turned his bones to liquid and his groin to steel, all so familiar and yet all so powerfully new.

Gently, he coaxed her lips apart and deepened the kiss,

deepened the craving that had never left him, had been banished to a dark recess until she came back into his life.

She moaned softly and parted her lips, digging her nails into his scalp.

For an age they stood there, swaying to the music, their mouths fused together, breathing each other in. The swaying bodies surrounding them disappeared into a haze; there but out of sight, the music reduced to a distant beat.

He wanted to consume her. He *needed* to consume her.

However much she might hate him, Grace belonged to him.

And he belonged to her.

A dancing couple inadvertently knocked into them.

Luca broke away with a muttered oath.

The room came swimming back into focus. Grace came swimming back into focus. She looked dazed, her eyes blinking furiously, her outward features exactly mirroring what he felt inside.

'Let's get out of here,' he said, taking her hand and tugging her off the dance floor.

She didn't resist. Indeed, she didn't say a word as they wove through the increasingly drunken revellers and out of the ballroom. Keeping a firm hold on her hand, he texted his driver to meet them at the front of the hotel.

Minutes later the driver opened the back door and they got inside.

'Take us back to our hotel,' Luca commanded.

Only when the limousine was moving and the privacy window had been erected did he turn to face her.

Her small chest heaved with short, ragged breaths. There was a wildness in her eyes, something feral seeping out of her pores.

'Come here.' His voice thick, he snaked a hand around her neck and pulled her to him.

She didn't need to be told twice. She pounced onto his lap and threw her arms around him.

Their lips came back together and he leaned back into the plush leather upholstery, cradling her head tenderly as he did so.

He had no idea what the nectar of myths and fables tasted like but knew it could never be sweeter than his wife's kisses. The most potent aphrodisiac could never evoke the desire one kiss from her could unleash.

Grace was the most openly sensuous woman he had ever known with a sex drive that perfectly matched his own. She'd never feigned coyness and what she initially lacked in experience she had more than made up for in enthusiasm. He had loved that raw honesty about her. The first time she had taken him into her mouth she'd knelt before him and fixed those hazel eyes on him. 'I've never done this before,' she'd said matter-of-factly. 'So sorry if I do it all wrong.'

It had ended up being one of the most incredible experiences of his life.

Now, as she straddled him with the earthy hunger he had always adored, he wondered how he had ever managed without her, without making love to her. Whether their couplings were short and frantic or long and luxurious, they would always end sated and content, locked in each other's arms.

Finally he broke away for air and razed his teeth down her neck, darting his tongue on the lobe of her ear. She moaned lightly and rubbed her cheek against his, her hands creeping down the plane of his chest and tugging his shirt loose so she could burrow under it.

It suddenly dawned on him that they were making out in the back of a car like a pair of adolescent teenagers.

He shifted slightly, then immediately wished he hadn't as his straining erection rubbed against the apex of her thighs.

'Enough,' he said roughly. He grabbed her hips and manoeuvred her so only her legs lay draped over his lap. It did absolutely nothing to ease the ache in his groin. 'I am not going to make love to you in the back of a car.'

She looked at him with eyes that were wickedly dazed. 'Why not?'

A bubble of laughter rose in his throat. Grace had perfected mock innocence into a fine art. 'Because we're not teenagers and there are two perfectly good beds waiting for us just minutes away.'

She pouted. 'Spoilsport.'

'Have I not taught you anything? Anticipation heightens pleasure.' He reached over and pulled the straps of her dress back up. 'You can choose the bed.'

'You're letting me choose something?'

'Don't start,' he warned, before deciding it was easier to cut an argument off at the bud rather than let it bloom into something bigger by kissing her again.

'I thought we weren't going to make out in the back of a car,' she murmured between kisses.

'I make the rules.' He covered her mouth again in another long, delicious kiss.

Without his being fully aware of it, her hand had burrowed back up his shirt. She pinched a nipple. 'That's what you think.'

Before he could respond she had twisted her body to climb back on top of him.

Just as he was starting to think there was something to be said for acting like a lust-driven teenager, the limo came to a stop.

She lifted her head and peered through the window. 'Oh.... We're back at the hotel.'

Wrapping an arm around her neck, he pulled her down for one last kiss. 'What did I tell you about anticipation?'

When the driver opened the door to let them out, they were sitting respectably, side by side, thighs pressed together, hands clasped.

Hand in hand, they strode through the hotel lobby, their minders, who had been in the car behind them, having to hurry to keep pace. Luca could only hope no one was paying enough attention to notice the enormous erection straining through his trousers, or spotted that more of Grace's orange lipstick covered her face than her lips.

For Grace, the journey up in the private elevator was little more than torture, the presence of the lift's concierge preventing her from doing anything more than cling to Luca's hand. If she had any doubts about what they were about to do, it was too late. The charge had become an inferno.

The second they were in the privacy of their suite, she was in his arms, her hands wrapped round his neck, drinking kisses that scorched, firing her blood.

Luca pushed her against the wall by the door and pressed against her, a hand tracing up her thigh and bunching the skirt of her dress up to her waist.

'Grace,' he groaned huskily, nipping at her bottom lip before reclaiming her mouth, his fingers playing at the rim of her knickers.

She slipped a hand down the front of his shirt, all the way down to his trousers, lower, until she reached the hardness of his erection. A noise came from his throat, almost a groan, a husky sound that speared her skin. Quickly, she undid the button and pulled the zip down, tugging his trousers and snug boxers down past his hips, allowing him to spring free. With fervoured hands, she held his length and rubbed a thumb over the head, rediscovering the hard, velvet smoothness. If ever an erection was beautiful, Luca's was it. Once she had made him lie on their bed naked, cajoled him with her mouth and tongue until he was as solid as rock then, with a wicked grin, had backed away and sketched him.

Now she had no intention of backing away.

Forget a bed. Forget foreplay. Forget everything. *It had been so long.*

She gasped as her knickers were ripped off and discarded, and when he inserted a finger into her sodden warmth she moaned and ground herself against him, wanting more, *needing* more.

All she wanted was to feel him deep inside her, filling her and fulfilling her as only Luca could, and she almost screamed in frustration when he moved his hand away and reached round to clench her buttocks, lifting her off her feet.

Immediately she released her hold on him and grabbed his shirt, pulling him so he was flush against her.

He broke their kiss and stared at her with a hungry, animalistic look, his eyes devouring her. 'You are the sexiest woman on the planet,' he said, the words coming out as a growl before he smothered her mouth.

Gripping one of her thighs, he raised it, giving her the extra lift she needed to wrap her legs around his waist, his strength supporting them both.

In one sure move he was inside her.

She cried out his name, tearing her mouth from his, biting his earlobe. There was no time to savour the feeling because it wasn't enough. Not nearly enough. All the cells inside her felt ready to explode.

Clinging to him, she buried her face in his shoulder and breathed in his musky scent, nipping at the salty flesh.

It was as if they'd never been apart, their bodies perfectly in tune to the other's needs. And what they both needed was release.

She met every carnal thrust as if it were the last, could

feel the pulsations within her core thicken. Luca's groans deepened and she knew his control was hanging by a thread, something she had always revelled in, the knowledge that this sexy bear of a man wanted her so badly. He knew her body as well as if it were an extension of his own. By pushing her thighs apart just a little and raising her slightly higher against the wall, he deepened the penetrations.

And then she was there. Closing her eyes tightly, she ground into him, her climax careering through her like a cresting wave, the ripples spreading out into every cell from the ends of her toes to the tips of her fingers and up to the strands of her hair.

He plunged into her with one final thrust, before losing his control with a cry, breathing heavily into her hair as together they wrung out every last millimetre of pleasure.

For an age they stayed that way, holding on to each other tightly until the spasms subsided and clarity broke through the haze.

Reluctant though she was to break the union, Grace's legs became limp and unfurled from around him.

Luca laughed lightly and withdrew from inside her, holding her waist securely while she found her feet.

'Okay?' he asked, brushing his lips to her neck.

'I think so.' She wrapped her arms more tightly around him and swayed into his chest, nestling her head into his shoulder. She could feel the thud of his heart reverberating through him, and gave a wistful sigh at the familiarity.

His hands brushed the length of her back. 'Your bed or mine?'

Tilting her head, she met his midnight stare, her heart catching at the warmth in it, and the gleaming heat that was of a very different nature.

As dangerous as she knew it would be to actually spend

a night sharing a bed, sharing even more intimacy with him, she didn't care. At least not then. If she regretted it in the morning, then…well, then she would deal with it in the morning.

'Mine.'

Taking great care not to disturb him, Grace disentangled her limbs from Luca's and crept out of bed.

After making love again, he had pulled her into his arms and fallen asleep. Usually the sound of his deep, steady breathing was enough to pull her into slumber too but tonight her brain refused to switch off. Which was hardly surprising under the circumstances.

Padding out of the bedroom, she headed into the main room of the suite and began rummaging through the bureau. There, she found an A4-sized notepad and an expensive-looking fountain pen with a variety of nibs and ink cartridges. She hardly cared. Her fingers were itching worse than any itch she could recall. She would have been satisfied with a lip liner.

Back in the bedroom she turned the small light of the dressing table down to its dimmest setting, quietly dragged the armchair to the side of the bed and nestled into it.

She had no idea how long she had been drawing when Luca's deep voice broke through the silence. 'Have you given me horns?'

She raised her eyes from the pad on her lap and threw a sheepish smile. Shoving her hand down her side, she pulled out a crumpled piece of paper and threw it at him.

He sat up, unfurled the paper and smoothed it out. He looked from the paper to her and back again. There was no anger in his expression, more a sad acceptance. But that could easily have been a trick of the light.

She'd sketched him sleeping. The more detail she'd put

into it, the tighter her chest had become. The longer she had drawn, the more the hate inside her had continued to squeeze out, and so, in desperation, she had drawn a thick, narrow goatee on his chin, quickly followed by a set of intricate horns above his ears. She'd even popped a red cartridge into the pen to tint the eyes, the only colour on the page. When she'd finished, her gaze had flittered between the devil on the page and the devil on the bed. Except her eyes no longer recognised the devil on the bed for what it was. All she could see was the man, sleeping, strangely innocent in his slumber. Her heart had clenched so tightly her eyes had brimmed. And she'd looked back down on that page and it had felt all wrong.

Screwing it into a tight ball, she'd started again, using nothing but her eyes to dictate what her hands drew. This picture felt cleaner somehow.

'If it's any consolation, the picture I'm drawing now is definitely *sans* horns.' Despite her best efforts she couldn't hide the catch in her throat.

'It is,' he said, his voice thick.

She looked up.

'It is a consolation,' he clarified, a wry smile playing on his lips.

She dropped her gaze back to the pad on her lap and added some strokes to thicken the hair. 'Are you ready to tell me about the breakup of your partnership with Francesco Calvetti?'

Her question seemed to surprise him, catching him mid yawn. 'There's not much to say. I have decided now is the right time to break it.'

Dropping a tiny splodge of ink along the jaw, she rubbed it with her middle finger to represent the dark stubble of his jawline. 'But why now?'

'There are many reasons.'

Silence hung in the air.

'How did you come to work with him in the first place? You never did tell me.' She kept her voice calm and non-accusatory. The soft lighting in the dark room had created a peaceful ambiance and she wanted to keep it that way, reluctant to spoil the harmony they had created, however fleeting that harmony might be.

Expelling a deep breath, Luca swung his legs off the bed and strode to the window, drawing back the curtains.

With his back to her, his naked torso had never looked more magnificent.

Quickly she turned the page of her pad over and started on a fresh sheet.

She waited for him to speak.

'Our fathers were great friends as well as associates. Francesco and I went to school together, spent time on holiday together, that kind of thing.'

'Really? I vaguely remember him from our wedding, but until you went into business with him when you bought the first casino, I didn't even know his name.' And then they had bought another casino and then the nightclubs. It hadn't taken long before she had grown to hate the name Francesco Calvetti.

'Francesco's father was a bastard.'

She paused, saying nothing, letting him fill the silence.

'If you wanted to know what a proper gangster looked like, you would have looked no further than Salvatore Calvetti. He made the de' Medici look like pussy-cats.'

She could hear the disgust in his voice.

The frozen pen on the page had blotted and she whipped it away, rubbing her thumb over the blot, transforming it into shading down the arch of his back.

'The older Salvatore got, the more vicious he became. My father was very different. Age mellowed him. It was no surprise to any of us when he decided to break the association. He wanted to take what *you* would call a more… legitimate path, especially with Pepe and I at an age to follow in his footsteps. The estate had been in the family for generations and had always been a good source of income. My father decided it was time to realise its full potential and turn the vineyard into the pride of the country.'

'And Salvatore was happy to break their…association?'

'No. Only the fact they had been close friends since childhood allowed him to break away without any repercussions.' He placed his hands on the window-sill and stretched a leg back, peering out. 'My father died barely a year later. Pepe and I agreed we would follow his wishes and run the estate free from Salvatore's influence.'

'Did Salvatore try and muscle in?'

'Naturally. He felt it was his right.' His tone became menacing. 'But we set him straight.'

'Is that why the estate is protected like Fort Knox?'

He nodded. 'It had always been highly guarded, but after my father's death I thought it prudent to add extra security measures. I was not prepared to let that bastard anywhere near my family or our home and business. And God knows, he tried.'

'So, when you took over the estate, the business consisted of just that—the estate?'

'We already had the vineyards and olive groves.'

'But only on the Mastrangelo estate.'

He nodded.

Her mind reeled as she considered what her husband had accomplished in the thirteen years before she met him. It wasn't just the expansion, although, considering they now owned dozens of estates in eight European countries and a couple in South America, the expansion was no small feat.

Mastrangelo wine was world famous and had won every

prestigious award going. Mastrangelo olive oil came at a premium and was the oil of choice for discerning chefs in all corners of the globe.

Yes, Pepe had come on board once he had graduated, but Luca had been the driving force behind it all.

'If you hate Salvatore so much, how come you ended up in business with his son?'

'He died a few weeks after our first wedding anniversary.'

'Ah.' Hazily she recalled him mentioning an old family acquaintance passing away, remembered the way his lips had curved in a manner she had been unable to discern.

'You didn't want me at the funeral.' When she'd offered to go with him, Luca had rebuffed her; the first time in the whole of their marriage he had attended anything that could be classed as even vaguely social without her.

'I didn't want you anywhere near that bastard even if he was in a coffin. Pepe and I only went to assure ourselves he really was dead.'

'Is that when you and Francesco reconnected?'

'Yes. Francesco's relationship with Salvatore was difficult to say the least, but he showed his father great loyalty. Salvatore's death freed him to take his own path.'

'And his own path included working with you.'

'Only in certain areas. In some businesses it is good to spread the risk.' He sighed. 'I was only twenty-one when I took over the running of the Mastrangelo estate. This gave me a chance to spread my wings too.'

'Pepe didn't agree?'

'Pepe and Francesco have loathed each other for years—they fell out over a woman. I was at university when it happened. I forget the details.' Luca raised his broad shoulders. 'I am my own man. I do not need my brother's permission or blessing to do anything. Francesco is his own man too. He is not his father. What he proposed made a great deal of financial sense and earned us both a lot of money.'

'If it earned you so much money, why break the association?'

'It is the right time. I shall keep the restaurants—they practically run themselves—but the casinos and nightclubs are nocturnal activities and require a lot of hands-on involvement. I have a child now who is deserving of my time and attention. I want to be there for her bath times, I want to read her stories. I want to be a proper father to her.'

Lucky Lily, she thought, as an unexpected wave of desolation streamed through her.

There was a truism in the saying that you couldn't miss what you'd never had. And Grace hadn't missed her father during his long absences—even when he was at home, Graham's mind was always on worthier causes. She'd known he loved her and that had been enough. She'd known her mother loved her and that had been enough.

Or so she'd told herself.

She'd never pushed either of them on it. She'd simply accepted the situation with her parents for what it was, never allowing herself to consider it in any real depth, too fearful of what the answers might be—that her mother's art and her father's good causes were more important to them than their only child.

She'd never properly pushed Luca about what was *really* going on in his life either, too fearful to probe too deeply—she hadn't wanted to know the truth, only confronting the reality when her pregnancy had left her no choice.

She hadn't stuck around to confront him with the undeniable truth, which had scared and horrified her. Instead, she had run away without even giving him the basic opportunity to defend himself...

'And is that the only reason you're breaking the association?' she asked him softly. 'Because you want to spend time with Lily?'

He turned his head to look at her, his spine straightening. 'What other reason could there be?'

She shrugged. 'I guess I thought—hoped—it was because you realised what you had become.'

His eyes hardened. 'And what might that be?'

'Everything your father never wanted you to be.'

She regretted the words the moment they left her lips.

Luca barely flinched but that small movement was enough for her to know she'd hit a nerve.

He sucked in a breath and turned his back to her.

Feeling like the worst person in the world, she got up from the chair and joined him at the window. In silence they looked out at the *Piazza del Duomo*. Under normal circumstances, the starlit cathedral would fill her with joy and contentment. But not tonight. Even though she knew she had been right in what she had said, it had been cruel.

How incongruous was that? Just twenty-four hours ago she would have snatched at an opportunity to hurt him.

'I'm sorry, Luca,' she said quietly, placing a hand on his shoulder. 'That wasn't fair of me.'

When he didn't answer, just gazed out of the window, his jaw clenched, she pressed on. 'I don't want another argument. I know my thoughts and opinions don't mean jack to you, but I'll say it anyway—I'm pleased you've broken your association with that man. It makes me feel safer knowing he's no longer in your life.'

It seemed to take for ever for him to break out of his trance.

Slipping away from her, he said, 'It's late. We have an early flight to catch. I'll get some sleep in my own room.'

Biting her lip, she let him go.

Her heart heavy, she turned out the light and got into bed. The thick duvet felt cold without him.

CHAPTER TWELVE

LUCA UNLOCKED THE door of the cottage and switched on the light. Immediately the studio went from darkness to bright, bright light.

Closing the door behind him, his head aching, his chest tight, he paced to the far end of the room where Grace kept her paintings neatly stacked.

This was something he had done on many occasions during her absence, especially in the lonely nights when his bones had always felt cold whatever the outside temperature. He'd examined every one of her paintings, like a detective trying to find clues, seeing if there was anything in them that would even hint at why she had left him.

But it had been more than a mere forensic examination. He'd felt closer to her in there, her personality and spirit etched in her work. If he closed his eyes he could imagine her standing before her easel, her head tilted, her face screwed in concentration.

He sank to his knees to look through the paintings for what had to be the hundredth time and now, finally, he began to see.

Her early paintings had been vivid. She'd painted him, his family and many of the estate workers individually; beautiful, colourful pictures with personality and gusto. There were plenty of celebrity pieces too. He remembered how she would scour magazines, her excitement when she found a picture that 'jumped out' at her. She would cut it out and hurry to her easel, her mind already working overtime. The finished article would be nothing like the original photo but the person in question would never be in doubt.

As the length of their marriage increased, he could see a difference. Nothing obvious, not at first, but if you placed the pictures in chronological order… The later paintings were more muted, as if the vibrancy that lived inside her and extended into her artwork had dimmed.

It was the very last painting he had struggled the most to comprehend, the one left on her easel. The oil had still been wet when she vanished. Unlike her other portraits, which were always human, she had painted a black bird in flight, surrounded by a thin mist. He didn't recognise the breed, guessed she had created it from her own imagination.

For almost a year he had studied that bird, his mind ticking with increased desperation to see what, if anything, it represented. No matter how hard he looked, all he could see was a bird in flight.

Now, for the first time, he could see what he had been missing.

What he had assumed to be a thin mist he could now see was a dome. The bird was trying to fly out of the dome. The bird could see the freedom of the big wide world but was trapped within its cage.

The painting *was* a portrait. It was a self-portrait.

Grace had represented herself as the bird. Luca was the dome.

He staggered back to his feet, disconcerted to find the room swimming before his eyes.

It felt as if the walls were closing in on him.

Resting a hand against the wall, he took deep breaths to steady himself but found his airway restricted.

Dear God, what had he done?

He'd captured a beautiful, vibrant bird and taken away its freedoms and the very vivacity that had made it so special.

And then he had recaptured it and, instead of learning his lesson and nurturing it, he had tethered it ever closer, giving it no chance to spread its wings.

Was this really what he wanted? For Grace's wings to become so clipped she forgot what it even felt like to fly?

And was this what he wanted for Lily, his beautiful fledgling? A life of restriction? Of fear?

An image of his father came into his head, an image that had been fighting for space within him for days.

Grace had been right in her assessment. His father *would* be appalled to see the man his son had become. He had been fooling himself to ever think otherwise. Never minding his treatment of Grace, his father would be saddened that his eldest son seemed to have embraced the very things he had spent the last years of his life rejecting, the very things he had tried to steer his sons away from.

How had he sleepwalked into such a situation? The worst of it all was, deep down, he had known almost from the beginning that he had made a mistake. Instead of holding his hands up and bowing out, he had let his stupid pride take over, allowed the glamour of the establishments to seduce him, and invested in the nightclubs too.

Francesco might have despised Salvatore and abhorred anything to do with drugs or arms trafficking, but he had learned more than a few of his father's old tricks.

Luca remembered the first person they had caught trying to steal from their casino. Francesco's men had half killed him, and for what? All that man had tried to steal was a couple of hundred euros.

Why had he not put a stop to the beating?

It was a question he had asked himself hundreds of times.

He was not averse to violence when absolutely necessary—it was the only language many of the men he dealt with knew—but for two hundred euros? A swift kick in the ribs would have sent just as clear a message.

That night, he'd got home in the early hours and downed a long shot of Scotch before seeking Grace out in her studio. He remembered, clearly, finding her fast asleep in the bedroom, clambering under the sheets and pulling her to him.

His mind had still been reeling, his heart still racing from the assault he had witnessed. In his wife's loving arms he'd found some respite and oblivion.

After that first time, he'd left the security side of things in Francesco's hands with the assertion that his partner's men were to keep all physical damage proportionate and never to the point of no return. Ensuring his wishes were respected meant keeping a very close eye on proceedings.

Knowing no person would be killed in his name allowed him to sleep a little easier.

But as time had gone on, his sleep had become worse. It seemed as if every week someone was caught stealing from them or harassing their female staff. Then there were the drug dealers to contend with, always there, wanting to set up shop in their establishments. These scumbags he had no problem with being dealt with physically. They were nasty, malevolent creatures who deserved everything they got and he would happily throw the odd punch in himself.

These people had to be dealt with, to be taught a lesson that everyone else would understand. Even the petty thieves.

He had let it happen. He had let blood be spilled and bones broken, and told himself he was the force for good within the partnership. Usually he would tell himself that with a large glass of Scotch in hand.

If he thought it was so good, then why had he never shared any of it with Grace? It wasn't simply to do with protecting her or because she wouldn't understand. It was because he had known damn well she would be horrified, had known deep down that her happiness was becoming muted, the constraints of their life wearing her down.

He hadn't wanted to see the horror and disapproval that would have been sure to follow in her eyes.

He hadn't wanted to admit to his wife—even less to himself—that he had taken a wrong turn and was in so deep he could see no way out.

He hadn't wanted to give her any more of an excuse to leave because, out of everything, that was what he'd feared the most—that if he confided the truth of what was bearing down on his conscience, she would turn around and leave him.

And she had. Grace had learned the truth and left him.

Three years ago he'd had everything: a vivacious, beautiful wife who loved and understood him, a flourishing business, more money than he could ever spend in a lifetime…

The business and the money were still there but he'd thrown the rest away.

Grace was the best thing that had happened to him and he'd ruined it with his pride and selfishness. He had brought a danger and violence into their lives that were far more potent than any threat Salvatore had brought.

He staggered over to the large mirror she kept on a stand close to her easel, which she used for looking at her paintings with a different perspective.

His own perspective had altered too.

That sketch she had drawn of him was as close to real life as it was possible to get.

She had been right all along.

He really was the devil. An evil monster.

The weight of reality pushed down hard on his chest, its tentacles spreading out and pulling at him, making his skin tight and his stomach cramp.

He couldn't bear to look at his reflection for a second longer.

With a guttural roar, he ripped the mirror off the stand and threw it onto the terracotta floor, where it landed with a deafening crash.

With deep, ragged breaths he gazed at the shards of mirror scattered around him. His distorted image now reflected off thousands of tiny fragments.

The act was not enough to silence the demons screaming in his head or quell the sickness inside.

There were not enough mirrors in the world to purge him.

He didn't deserve to be purged.

In desperation he spun around, helpless for the first time since his father had died when he'd felt so hollow, as if the heart of him had been ripped out. This felt so much worse.

A sound behind him made him whip around again.

For the blink of an eye he was certain he had conjured her.

'Luca?' Grace said, approaching him with soft footsteps. 'What are you doing in here?'

He tried to move his throat but no words would form.

Her winter boots crunched on the scattered fragments and she froze, her eyes moving from him to the mess surrounding her. She looked back at him, her face creased with concern. 'I've been looking everywhere for you. Whatever is the matter?'

How could she even stomach looking at him, never mind looking at him as if she were *worried* about him?

He was not worthy of her compassion.

How could he have ever thought he hated her?

'Please, Luca,' she begged, crunching slowly towards him. 'Talk to me.'

How many times had she said those words?

How many times had he fobbed her off, refusing to admit to either of them that there was a problem?

What could he say now? Mere words could never convey the deluge of emotions raging through him or make up for everything he had put her through.

In a trice he closed the gap between them and cupped her cheeks in his palms. Her hazel eyes glittered and swirled but she made no attempt to break away, simply stared back as if trying to read his innermost thoughts.

He knew right there and then that he would have to let her and Lily go. He could not force the misery of this life and this unwanted marriage on her for a moment longer. But...

Before he set her free, he had the means to at least make partial atonement.

Closing his eyes, he brought his lips down on hers and held them there, breathing in the heady sweetness of her breath. He waited for a heartbeat, half expecting her to resist. Instead, her hands rose up his arms, bunching his sweater in her fists, and she swayed into him.

It was the sign he'd been waiting for.

Pulling her tightly into his arms, he kissed her hard, his heart expanding when she released her hold on his sweater and looped her arms around his neck, her responsive kisses as ardent as his own. Her fingers slipped into the neck of his shirt and scraped his skin, the warmth of her touch sending shivery tingles down his spine and lower into his groin.

'Upstairs,' he said, speaking into her mouth and sweeping her into his arms.

They had made love in her studio more times than he could ever hope to count, against the wall, on the worktop, on the sofa; pretty much everywhere.

When they had first married he had tried to carry her up the stairs of the cottage. Halfway up, they had collapsed in a fit of giggles and ended up making love right there, never making it to the bedroom.

This time, he carried her all the way. There was not the faintest trace of humour on her face, instead an almost fervoured seriousness he had rarely seen expressed by her.

The bedroom was cold.

He laid her down on the bed then crossed to the window and closed the curtains before flicking the heater on. Until it kicked into life and provided some warmth he would use his own body to warm her.

Her eyes didn't leave him. 'Luca,' she began, but he placed a finger to her lips to silence her.

'Not yet,' he whispered, kicking his shoes off and lying down next to her, replacing his finger with his mouth. She wrapped her arms around him and responded with the passion that was just one of the many things he had always loved about her. Their mouths merged into one, their tongues combining, their clad bodies clinging together, arms and hands stroking wherever they could reach.

Soon he broke away but only with his mouth, tracing his lips over her face, seeking every millimetre of silken skin from the lids of her eyes to the lobes of her ears. The soft moans escaping from her throat were like balm on a wound.

Only when he judged the room had warmed sufficiently that she would not freeze did he move away.

'Stay there,' he ordered, sealing his command with another kiss.

Her eyes had a dazed look about them, but she acquiesced with what could almost be called a contented sigh, stretching an arm over her head and staring at him.

In one swift movement he removed his sweater and threw it to the floor. Not taking his eyes off her, he quickly divested himself of his shirt, trousers and underwear until he was standing before her as naked as the day he had been born but with an erection that ached more than any he had ever known.

The powerful heater was already working its magic but he doubted he would have felt the cold.

Kneeling at the foot of the bed, he unlaced her boots and pulled them off along with her thick socks. Her feet were cold and he rubbed them in turn before dropping a gentle kiss on each toe.

Taking his time, he stripped her clothes, refusing all of her attempts to help. Soon, her jeans and bulky jumper were bundled in a pile on the floor like his own.

Aware this would be the last time he would see her naked, he let his eyes rake over her before following with his lips, determined to kiss and taste every last inch of her. Starting with her delectable mouth, his lips trailed down her neck and over her shoulders, his hands roaming free, exploring her smooth flesh.

Last night, when they had made love in Florence, their passion had been too frenzied to do anything more than touch, both too desperate for him to possess her to care much about foreplay.

Tonight, he could see all he had missed. The longer he kissed and explored, the more changes he found in her body, subtle differences from how he remembered her. Her nipples had darkened and her breasts, judging by the way she sucked in a breath and writhed beneath him when he took them in his mouth, had become even more sensitive.

She had always been naturally toned but now he could

see and feel a softness around her abdomen, as if a small cushion had been placed under her skin. Tiny red slivers ran under her belly button, more signs that she had recently carried a child—his child—inside her. He kissed every red mark reverently, fighting back an unexpected burn in the backs of his eyelids that threatened to break out when he thought of her going through pregnancy and birth alone.

How could he have ever judged her harshly for that, for protecting their child?

Tiny whimpers were coming from her throat. When he moved lower, down to her pelvis and the soft downy hair surrounding her pubis, she reached out and grabbed his hair, her fingers digging into his scalp.

He gently spread her legs. The moment he pressed his lips to her clitoris she gasped and tried to sit up. Holding her down with one hand on her belly, he buried his face there, his tongue rhythmically pressing against the nub of her pleasure, inhaling the musky scent he adored.

Her whimpers lengthened, deepening into groans. He opened his eyes and watched as her head rolled from side to side. Keeping his eyes fixed on her, he increased the pressure, moving the hand that had been holding her down upwards until he reached her breast and covered it.

Her back became rigid, almost lifting off the mattress as she climaxed. He kept his mouth and tongue exactly where they were until he was certain he had coaxed every ounce of pleasure from her. Then and only then did he snake his way back up, covering her belly and breasts with more kisses, his enormous erection rubbing against her thighs until he reached her mouth.

Her cheeks were flushed, her eyes aglow. Hooking an arm around his neck, she almost wrenched him down to kiss her mouth, her free hand trailing down his back to his buttocks.

And then he was inside her, deep within the hot moistness, the relief so great he almost came on the spot.

Closing his eyes, he took a deep breath and steadied himself. This, their last time together, was a moment to be cherished.

Grace had other ideas, raising her thighs for even deeper penetration, clinging to him, her mouth demanding ever more from his kisses.

It took everything he had to slow her down. He wanted—needed—to savour every minute. He wanted her to savour every minute too, to look back on this, their last time together, and think of him, if not with love, then something kinder than hate.

He withdrew, right to the tip, holding it there for as long as he could bear before pushing back inside. He let the motions increase a little with every thrust, until he established a steady tempo that had her whimpering anew, moaning his name, her hand clasping his buttocks, the fingers of her other hand scraping his scalp.

Only when he felt the muscles within her contract and her body go rigid did he finally allow himself to let go too, his cry of relief sounding like a roar as he made one final thrust, holding on to the moment for as long as he could before collapsing on top of her.

For what seemed an age, he lay there, buried inside her and on her, reluctant to move, desperate to hold on to the moment for as long as he could.

Eventually the chill on his back forced him to move.

It hadn't been the power of the heater that had warmed him earlier but the heat Grace created within him.

He covered them in the duvet and pulled her to him, his head already thickening with the need to sleep. One more sleep with her and then…

Grace sat bolt upright, jerking him awake.

'Your mum must be doing her nut!' she cried.

Before she could escape from the bed he trapped her wrist. 'What's the problem?'

'I put Lily to bed and then got your mum to watch over her so I could come and find you—I didn't think I'd be this long!'

'My mother will be fine,' he soothed, pulling her back to him.

'No, she won't. She's shattered.' She wriggled out from his hold and climbed off the bed. 'I think Lily must have kept her awake all night. I promised I wouldn't be long.'

'Why were you looking for me?'

'You missed Lily's bedtime. You haven't seen her since we got back. I knew you were home but I couldn't find you anywhere and you weren't answering your phone.' She looked up from the pile of clothes she was sorting through and threw him a wry smile. 'Maybe I should get a tracker put on it so I can keep tabs on *you*.'

He winced. Knowing he deserved it did not take away the sting.

His heart felt weighted as he watched her dress.

She must have felt him staring, pausing from yanking her jeans up. 'What's the matter?'

There was one question he needed to know the answer to before he let her go. 'Why did you stop painting?'

'I…' She hesitated. 'I'm not sure. I guess I was too busy running.'

'I'm sorry I never bought you a gallery.'

Her eyes widened a fraction.

'You were right—I didn't think it was safe enough outside the estate for you.'

Eyes still wide, she hooked her jumper over her head. When she came up for air she said, 'I was going to buy it for myself.'

'Really?' He was about to ask what money she would have used when it came to him in a flash. 'Your allowance.'

She nodded, smoothing the jumper down over her belly. 'It was just sitting in the bank doing nothing.'

'I wondered why you hadn't touched it.'

'I wasn't going to touch the allowance, not at first. I never wanted it in the first place.'

'So why accept it?'

'When I agreed to it we were in that soppy honeymoon phase. I knew refusing would hurt your feelings and I didn't want to do that. But then a few months before I left I got to thinking—why shouldn't I buy it? That money was mine to do as I wished.'

'But you knew buying it would go against my wishes?'

She slipped her feet into her boots and looked up at him. Her smile was sad. 'Actually, I didn't know that. You never said it in so many words; just evaded the topic every time I brought the subject up. But yes, I had a good idea you wouldn't approve.'

'Yet you were still prepared to go ahead and do it.'

'I like to think I would have. It was either that or hate you for your pig-headedness. I loved you. You were my world. But you were not my life. You knew when we married I had a mind of my own and that I'm not some insipid flower who wilts at the first sign of confrontation…' Her voice trailed off, her eyes becoming glazed.

'Grace?'

She blinked and gave a short shake of her head before continuing where she had left off. 'I knew opening my own gallery without your input would cause conflict between us but I thought—hoped—we were strong enough to overcome it.' She finished tying her laces and looked at her watch again. 'I really need to get back to your mum. Are you coming with me?'

'No. I'll get the mirror cleared up and then I have things I need to do.'

'Okay.' She bit her bottom lip, looking as if she was about to say something. Instead, she shook her head as if to shake an errant thought away. 'I'll see you later, then.'

Only when he was certain she had left the cottage did he slump forward and grip his head in his hands.

CHAPTER THIRTEEN

GRACE LISTENED OUT for Luca's return but the door to their wing remained resolutely closed all night. Lily hardly slept either. If she didn't know better, Grace could swear she was waiting for him to come home too.

Something was troubling him and her heart ached to reach out.

The way he had made love to her…it wasn't just the tenderness, it was the expression in his eyes, so much emotion.

As ridiculous as she knew it to be, it had felt as if he were saying goodbye.

Once Lily was up, fed and dressed, she decided to take her out for a walk. Maybe the crisp air could clear her head of the melancholy that had set in.

Just as she was about to push the pram into the woodland surrounding the monastery, a black Jeep came up the drive. Her heart jumped into her mouth but when it drove slowly past she saw it was one of the guards of the estate. Nonetheless, she waved politely, scolding herself for her irrational reaction. She shouldn't get all skittish at the thought she might see her husband. And her heart certainly should not be pounding because of it.

After an hour of traipsing through the woods and skirting round the vineyards, she headed back feeling every bit as jumbled as she had when she'd left.

At least the fresh air had done Lily some good. She'd fallen fast asleep.

Grace lifted her out of the pram and carried her into their wing. Even when she stripped her out of the thick snowsuit, Lily didn't make a murmur.

After settling her in the cot, Grace wandered back into her own room and saw she'd left her passport on her pillow.

'I must be cracking up,' she muttered under her breath, snatching it up, dislodging an envelope resting under it which she couldn't remember seeing before. She really was going bonkers. She could have sworn she'd put the passport in the top drawer of her dresser when they'd returned from Florence. Except, when she opened the said drawer she found her passport in the exact place she had left it.

She opened the new passport, took one look at the picture and dropped it as if scalded.

It belonged to Lily.

Hands shaking, she retrieved it from the floor and took another look. What the heck was it doing in her room…?

Clutching it to her chest, she wandered out into the corridor.

The master bedroom was empty.

The office door was closed. She nudged it open.

Luca was sitting behind his desk, dressed in the same clothes he'd been wearing when she'd found him in her studio.

He looked a mess, his hair sticking out all over the place, the stubble around his jaw thick.

He raised bloodshot eyes.

She held the passport out. 'I found this in my room.'

He groaned. 'I put it there.'

'You did? But why?'

'Isn't it obvious?'

'Not really.'

He dragged a hand down his face and exhaled slowly. 'You are free to take Lily and leave.'

Fearing her legs would give way beneath her, she leaned back against the door. 'Just like that?'

'Please, Grace, don't make this any harder than it is. Pack your things. I'll arrange for a driver to take you wherever you want to go. When you're ready, call me and we'll sort out the finances.'

She could not respond. She opened her mouth but nothing came out.

'I assume the cheque is adequate to get you started?'

When she continued to stare at him blankly, his forehead creased. 'I wrote a cheque out for you and left it with Lily's passport.'

'I never opened the envelope.'

He scratched his head, breathing deeply. 'If you find it isn't enough, just say and I'll write you another. Or you can give me your bank details and I'll transfer the money straight into it. Not that I would blame you if you didn't trust me with those details.'

Unexpected freedom was within her grasp. She could almost reach out and touch it but her brain was having trouble processing it. This was such an about-face it was hard to comprehend. 'Why are you doing this?'

'Because you don't belong here.'

His answer felt like a slap in the face.

He must have read her shock. 'You have never belonged here,' he said, utter dejection ringing from his eyes. 'The restrictions of my life, the security, my business dealings, all it did was stifle you.'

'You tried,' she said, feeling a strange compulsion to defend him from himself. 'You tried so hard to make me happy.'

He might have got cold feet about her having a proper

gallery away from the estate, but that did not take away from the wonderful studio he had created for her or the hours he had spent in there with her, bringing his work into her world so they could be together. She doubted there were many men who would be so tolerant of a wife prone to disappearing from the marital bed in the middle of the night to paint.

'Please, do not make excuses for me.' His hands balled into fists. 'I deserve nothing but your contempt. We both know you would have left me eventually, even if you hadn't become pregnant.'

'We don't know that.'

'*I do.* Being here was killing the essence of *you.* Sooner or later you would have had enough. Tell me the truth. Given a choice, would you want to live here? Would you want Lily to be brought up here?'

She shook her head, wishing with all her heart that she could lie to him.

Why wasn't she jumping up and down with glee?

Luca was handing her everything she wanted. Her and Lily's freedom.

He closed his eyes but not before she caught the bleakness that had flittered into them. 'You and Lily will be happier away from Sicily. You need somewhere with freedom, a thriving art community, sunlight and people. The only thing I can provide for you here is the sunlight.'

'But...'

'Grace, I should never have forced you back. I have many regrets—so numerous I'm going to spend the rest of my life doing good deeds if I'm to have any chance of avoiding hell—but my biggest regret is my treatment of you. I brought danger into our lives. I kept you a virtual prisoner...' His eyes snapped open to stare at the ceiling. 'Everything I have done has caused you harm. I've behaved like a monster and I do not blame you for wanting to raise our child away from my influence. I will leave it to you to decide if I am to be allowed any contact with her. Whatever you decide, know I will support both of you financially and know I am more sorry than I could ever express.'

She should turn around and go before he changed his mind.

'So that's it?' She needed to make sure. 'Lily and I can leave, right now, and never come back and never set foot in Sicily again and never see you again?'

He rubbed the back of his neck. When he answered it was full of weariness. 'If that is your wish, then yes.'

She believed him. She could grab her daughter and slam the door on Sicily and Luca for ever.

'Please, Grace.' His voice caught before he blew a puff of air out of his mouth. 'Please, leave now. Looking at you hurts my heart.'

'Okay,' she said uncertainly. 'I guess this is goodbye, then.'

He gave a curt nod, no longer looking at her. 'Goodbye, Grace.'

Taking a shuddering breath, she stepped over the threshold.

'If you or Lily need anything—anything at all—I'll always be here for you,' he spoke quietly after her.

Unexpected hot tears burned her eyes. She tried to walk to her room but every step felt as if ten-tonne slabs of concrete had been placed inside her limbs.

For an age she stood there, unable to move, the utter misery and dejection on Luca's face the only thing she could see when she closed her eyes.

He had fallen in love with Lily and he was still letting them go.

And he loved her, Grace, too. She could feel it in her

heart. Since he had come to her bedroom and spent the evening bathing and dressing their daughter, it was as if the old Luca had slipped back into his skin and slowly reclaimed his body.

He was giving her everything she wanted. Except for one thing…

Hadn't she realised that last night, after they'd made love? She would have been happy to buy a gallery knowing it would be against his wishes, but confrontation involving anything *real*, she backed away from.

Unless she put her heart on the line and fought for the one thing she wanted above all else, she would lose it for ever.

She hurried back into his office, her legs suddenly working just fine in her haste.

Luca was slumped over his desk, his face buried in a pile of papers.

'You said I could leave Sicily and never return if that were my wish. Well, what if my wish is for you to come with us?'

He slowly raised his head, a deep groove indented in his forehead.

She took a step towards him. 'What if Lily and I loved you so much we didn't want to be parted from you again?'

His mouth formed a tight line, his eyes not moving from her.

She moved closer. 'What if I were to tell you I stuck it out in Cornwall for longer than I knew was safe because a tiny part of me missed you so badly it wanted you to find me?' As she spoke the words she knew them to be true. That strange lethargy that had overcome her, that hollow feeling that something was missing…

The rational, protective part of her had been terrified of Luca discovering them.

Her irrational heart had ached for him.

'What if I were to tell you I couldn't paint because being without you made me so miserable, the creative part of me died?' Reaching him, she leaned against his desk and took one of his trembling hands. 'What if,' she continued, turning it palm up and pressing a kiss to it, 'what if I were to ask you to start again, somewhere new? Would you do it? Would you be prepared to move and run the estate from a different country if it meant we could be together as a family?'

He reached out to palm her cheek with his free hand, gazing intently into her eyes. The groove on his forehead had vanished. '*Mio Dio*, you're serious.'

The tears she had been holding back spilled over. She wiped them away. Right at that moment tears were a nuisance; she didn't want to cry when she was about to say the most important words of her life. 'You're right. I don't belong here but I do belong with *you*. I've told you about my childhood and what it was like—I was wanted and loved but I never felt that, that…' She struggled to find the right words. 'I guess I always felt separate from my parents. I have *never* felt separate from you, even when we were apart—you were with me for every second of it. I love you, Luca, and I don't think I could bear to be parted from you again.'

He had her on his lap and wrapped in his arms so quickly she had no time to even blink.

Her head pressed against his chest, he held her tightly, breathing deeply into her hair. '*Dio*, I never thought I would ever hear you say that again.'

'Nor did I.' She tilted her head and raised a hand to stroke his cheek. 'I love you.'

'I don't deserve your love.'

Another tear rolled down her cheek and she gave an

impish smile. 'I know. But what can you do?' She straightened so she was face to face with him. 'And you can't put everything on yourself.'

The furrow on his forehead reappeared. 'What do you mean?'

'I'm your wife. I *knew* something was wrong and I should have pushed harder to make you talk to me.'

'Grace, it would have made no difference. I couldn't confide in you. Not then. I was in too deep and too frightened of losing you to think straight.'

'I should have at least tried. But I was too scared.'

Consternation crossed his face. 'Of me? I would *never* raise a—'

'No!' She cut him off sharply. 'I know you would never so much as lift a finger against me. No. I was scared to confront the truth. I was scared that if my suspicions were proven correct then I would have to ask you to choose between me and your association with Francesco. I could never have condoned what you two were doing, whatever the reasoning behind it. I couldn't have lived with it—I just couldn't.' Her voice dropped to a whisper. 'I didn't believe you would choose me.'

She had trusted his love but she hadn't trusted that it was strong enough to put her first. She could see that now. She had spent her entire life feeling that her parents' love for her was secondary to their lives. To her, that kind of love had been normal.

'Ah, *amore*,' he groaned before pressing his head against hers and breathing in deeply. 'I would never choose anyone or anything over you.'

'And maybe if I'd believed that, I would have forced you to confide in me as soon as the warning signs were there that something was wrong. We don't know if things would have turned out differently, and that's what I mean when I say you can't put it all on yourself.'

Luca expelled a breath slowly, the warm air from his lungs tickling her hair.

Grace took her own deep breath. 'So what would you say? If I asked you to abandon your life here and come with us, would you?'

He kissed her forehead almost reverentially. 'I would follow you to the ends of the earth if I thought that was what you wanted.'

She closed her eyes at the suffusion of warmth his words provided.

'But is it what *you* want?' Doubts suddenly crowded her as she thought of what she was really asking of him—to give up the only life he had ever known.

'All I want is you and Lily. Being without you...Grace, I cannot begin to tell you how lost I felt. And you're right. This life here is no kind of life. Not for you.'

'It's your life though.' Now she thought about it, she could see the total abandonment of Sicily would never work. 'There's so much to think about.' She sighed. 'Too much of your life and business is tied up here.'

'The majority of the wine and olive business is in Europe,' he mused. 'Francesco's buying out my share of the casinos and nightclubs, which will free me up to base myself anywhere I choose, like Pepe.'

'But this is your home. How would your mum feel if we moved away? She'd be heartbroken.'

'My mum is as tough as old Parma ham.'

She sniggered. 'I know, but she adores Lily. She can always come with us.'

He pulled away and stared at her quizzically. 'Seriously? You would want my mother to come with us?'

'I know she's never approved of me but she is your mother and she does love Lily.'

'She *does* approve of you,' he insisted. 'She's always thought you were wonderful but she could see from the beginning that the restrictions of living here would wear you down. And she was right.'

She snuggled back into his chest, a warm feeling of contentment seeping through her bones ridding her of the final vestiges of poison.

'We'll work it out,' he promised, stroking her hair. 'As long as we're together, and as long as we're talking to each other about the things that matter, we'll figure it out.'

'Did you know I managed to escape your goons' X-ray vision for all of two minutes and buy a new untracked phone?'

He laughed and rubbed his chin on her hair. 'Now why doesn't that surprise me?'

Snickering, she buried her face in his chest, catching a whiff of stale alcohol. 'Have you been drinking?'

His voice became rueful. 'I stayed the night in your studio nursing the best part of a bottle of Scotch.'

'Were you very drunk?'

'No. Believe me, I tried very hard to find oblivion. I knew what I had to do but I was delaying the inevitable.'

'I can't believe you were prepared to let me go.'

'And I can't believe what a bastard I was in forcing you to stay, and I can't believe you're prepared to give me another chance. I swear, I'll never give you cause to regret it.'

'As long as you promise to stay away from any business venture involving Francesco Calvetti.'

'You can't blame Francesco. I am my own man and I make my own choices. But I promise from now on all my business ventures will be legitimate in the sense that *you* recognise.'

'Good. You must also swear there will be no more secrets between us.'

'No more secrets.'

She rubbed her nose into his neck, catching another scent, a very faint trace of his new cologne. 'Why did you change your aftershave? I thought another woman had bought it for you.'

His laugh was savage. 'There has been no one else. I changed it because every time I smelt the old one it reminded me of you and made me miss you so much it hurt.'

'Good. Because you must also swear to never, ever, *ever* even think about taking a mistress.'

'As long as I'm breathing you are the only woman for me. You. Just you.'

'Good. Because if you went with another woman I swear to God I'd rip your heart out.'

'My heart would have to be ripped out for me to stop loving and wanting you.' He bent his head and brushed his lips to hers. 'I never stopped loving you, even when you shot me.'

Her laugh was shaky. 'And I never stopped loving you, even when I hated you.'

'No more hate.' His lips parted and he pulled her into a kiss of such tender sweetness that the last hollow patch inside her belly filled and made her whole.

EPILOGUE

THE MONASTERY WAS filled with friends and family, the Mastrangelo contingent of aunts, uncles and cousins far outweighing the handful that had flown over for the occasion from England. Lily Elizabeth Mastrangelo had been baptised earlier in the same church in Lebbrossi where Grace and Luca had married. The beaming congregation had all agreed she was the most beautiful baby to bless the earth—although Grace could have sworn one of the small Mastrangelo cousins had likened Lily to a pig, but her language skills were so pathetic it was likely a mistranslation.

Donatella approached her, a glass of red wine in hand. 'Aunt Carlotta has kidnapped Lily,' she said, looking more relaxed than Grace had ever seen her.

'I don't think I've seen her since we got back from the church.' Grace laughed. 'The relatives have been too busy playing Pass the Baby.'

'I'm going to miss her,' Donatella admitted with a rueful smile.

'I know. It's not too late—you can still come with us.'

'Thank you for the offer but my home is in Sicily.'

'It's not as if Rome's the other side of the world. You can visit whenever you like and of course we'll make plenty of trips back here.' She and Luca had found the ideal compromise—half the year in Sicily and half the year in Rome.

She could live with that and so could Luca. Six months of hyper-security and six months of freedom and anonymity. It was a good compromise. Their new home in Rome now beckoned, waiting for their small family to move into it. Her fingers were already itching to get decorating.

Scanning the room for Luca, who had earlier disappeared to their personal wine cellar with a couple of uncles demanding a tour, she spotted Cara and Pepe having what looked to her eyes like a heated discussion. She'd already had a good chat with her friend but had found her distinctly cagey about how Pepe had got hold of her phone. So cagey, in fact, that she had refused to discuss it.

When Luca reemerged a short while later, she pulled him to one side. 'Do you know what's going on between those two?'

He looked over and shrugged. 'Pepe refuses to talk about it with me.'

As Lily's godparents, Cara and Pepe had been required to stand together during the baptism. Grace had noticed the way Cara had refused to even look at him. Now her sweet-natured friend looked as if she wanted to rip his throat out.

'Leave them to get on with it,' Luca advised, clearly reading her mind. Standing behind her, he wrapped his arms around her waist and rested his chin on the top of her head. 'We have guests to mingle with, Signora Mastrangelo, before we can slope off for an early night.'

She didn't have to be a mind-reader to know what was on his mind. She could feel the bulge in his trousers resting in the small of her back.

'The day has worn me out,' she said with faux innocence, pressing back into him so they were completely flush. 'An early night is just what I need.'

'Seeing as it's our last night here, we should get my mum to look after Lily.'

'That would be the nice thing to do. After all, she won't get woken up in the middle of the night by a teething baby for *ages*.'

'We'll be doing her a favour really.'

'Absolutely,' she agreed, heat already bubbling in her veins at the thought of what the night would bring.

* * * * *

Mills & Boon® Hardback

March 2014

ROMANCE

A Prize Beyond Jewels	Carole Mortimer
A Queen for the Taking?	Kate Hewitt
Pretender to the Throne	Maisey Yates
An Exception to His Rule	Lindsay Armstrong
The Sheikh's Last Seduction	Jennie Lucas
Enthralled by Moretti	Cathy Williams
The Woman Sent to Tame Him	Victoria Parker
What a Sicilian Husband Wants	Michelle Smart
Waking Up Pregnant	Mira Lyn Kelly
Holiday with a Stranger	Christy McKellen
The Returning Hero	Soraya Lane
Road Trip With the Eligible Bachelor	Michelle Douglas
Safe in the Tycoon's Arms	Jennifer Faye
Awakened By His Touch	Nikki Logan
The Plus-One Agreement	Charlotte Phillips
For His Eyes Only	Liz Fielding
Uncovering Her Secrets	Amalie Berlin
Unlocking the Doctor's Heart	Susanne Hampton

MEDICAL

Waves of Temptation	Marion Lennox
Risk of a Lifetime	Caroline Anderson
To Play with Fire	Tina Beckett
The Dangers of Dating Dr Carvalho	Tina Beckett

0214GEN STD HB

ROMANCE

Million Dollar Christmas Proposal	Lucy Monroe
A Dangerous Solace	Lucy Ellis
The Consequences of That Night	Jennie Lucas
Secrets of a Powerful Man	Chantelle Shaw
Never Gamble with a Caffarelli	Melanie Milburne
Visconti's Forgotten Heir	Elizabeth Power
A Touch of Temptation	Tara Pammi
A Little Bit of Holiday Magic	Melissa McClone
A Cadence Creek Christmas	Donna Alward
His Until Midnight	Nikki Logan
The One She Was Warned About	Shoma Narayanan

HISTORICAL

Rumours that Ruined a Lady	Marguerite Kaye
The Major's Guarded Heart	Isabelle Goddard
Highland Heiress	Margaret Moore
Paying the Viking's Price	Michelle Styles
The Highlander's Dangerous Temptation	Terri Brisbin

MEDICAL

The Wife He Never Forgot	Anne Fraser
The Lone Wolf's Craving	Tina Beckett
Sheltered by Her Top-Notch Boss	Joanna Neil
Re-awakening His Shy Nurse	Annie Claydon
A Child to Heal Their Hearts	Dianne Drake
Safe in His Hands	Amy Ruttan

0214 GEN STD LP

Mills & Boon® Hardback

April 2014

ROMANCE

A D'Angelo Like No Other	Carole Mortimer
Seduced by the Sultan	Sharon Kendrick
When Christakos Meets His Match	Abby Green
The Purest of Diamonds?	Susan Stephens
Secrets of a Bollywood Marriage	Susanna Carr
What the Greek's Money Can't Buy	Maya Blake
The Last Prince of Dahaar	Tara Pammi
The Sicilian's Unexpected Duty	Michelle Smart
One Night with Her Ex	Lucy King
The Secret Ingredient	Nina Harrington
Her Soldier Protector	Soraya Lane
Stolen Kiss From a Prince	Teresa Carpenter
Behind the Film Star's Smile	Kate Hardy
The Return of Mrs Jones	Jessica Gilmore
Her Client from Hell	Louisa George
Flirting with the Forbidden	Joss Wood
The Last Temptation of Dr Dalton	Robin Gianna
Resisting Her Rebel Hero	Lucy Ryder

MEDICAL

200 Harley Street: Surgeon in a Tux	Carol Marinelli
200 Harley Street: Girl from the Red Carpet	Scarlet Wilson
Flirting with the Socialite Doc	Melanie Milburne
His Diamond Like No Other	Lucy Clark

0314GEN STD HB

ROMANCE

Defiant in the Desert	Sharon Kendrick
Not Just the Boss's Plaything	Caitlin Crews
Rumours on the Red Carpet	Carole Mortimer
The Change in Di Navarra's Plan	Lynn Raye Harris
The Prince She Never Knew	Kate Hewitt
His Ultimate Prize	Maya Blake
More than a Convenient Marriage?	Dani Collins
Second Chance with Her Soldier	Barbara Hannay
Snowed in with the Billionaire	Caroline Anderson
Christmas at the Castle	Marion Lennox
Beware of the Boss	Leah Ashton

HISTORICAL

Not Just a Wallflower	Carole Mortimer
Courted by the Captain	Anne Herries
Running from Scandal	Amanda McCabe
The Knight's Fugitive Lady	Meriel Fuller
Falling for the Highland Rogue	Ann Lethbridge

MEDICAL

Gold Coast Angels: A Doctor's Redemption	Marion Lennox
Gold Coast Angels: Two Tiny Heartbeats	Fiona McArthur
Christmas Magic in Heatherdale	Abigail Gordon
The Motherhood Mix-Up	Jennifer Taylor
The Secret Between Them	Lucy Clark
Craving Her Rough Diamond Doc	Amalie Berlin

0314 GEN STD LP